WITCH'S FOREST

GIANTFUR CAVE
AND FALLEN TREE

ROCKY
OVERHANG

R

THE
COAST

SURVIVORS

STORM OF DOGS

Also by ERIN HUNTER

SURVIVORS

NOVELLAS

WARRIORS

THE NEW PROPHECY

POWER OF THREE
Book One: The Sight
Book Two: Dark River
Book Three: Outcast
Book Four: Eclipse
Book Five: Long Shadows
Book Six: Sunrise

OMEN OF THE STARS
Book One: The Fourth Apprentice
Book Two: Fading Echoes
Book Three: Night Whispers
Book Four: Sign of the Moon
Book Five: The Forgotten Warrior
Book Six: The Last Hope

DAWN OF THE CLANS
Book One: The Sun Trail
Book Two: Thunder Rising
Book Three: The First Battle
Book Four: The Blazing Star

EXPLORE THE
WARRIORS
WORLD

Warriors Super Edition: Firestar's Quest
Warriors Super Edition: Bluestar's Prophecy
Warriors Super Edition: SkyClan's Destiny
Warriors Super Edition: Crookedstar's Promise
Warriors Super Edition: Yellowfang's Secret
Warriors Super Edition: Tallstar's Revenge
Warriors Super Edition: Bramblestar's Storm

Warriors Field Guide: Secrets of the Clans
Warriors: Cats of the Clans
Warriors: Code of the Clans
Warriors: Battles of the Clans
Warriors: Enter the Clans
Warriors: The Ultimate Guide
Warriors: The Untold Stories
Warriors: Tales from the Clans

MANGA

The Lost Warrior
Warrior's Refuge
Warrior's Return
The Rise of Scourge
Tigerstar and Sasha #1: Into the Woods
Tigerstar and Sasha #2: Escape from the Forest
Tigerstar and Sasha #3: Return to the Clans
Ravenpaw's Path #1: Shattered Peace
Ravenpaw's Path #2: A Clan in Need
Ravenpaw's Path #3: The Heart of a Warrior
SkyClan and the Stranger #1: The Rescue
SkyClan and the Stranger #2: Beyond the Code
SkyClan and the Stranger #3: After the Flood

NOVELLAS

Hollyleaf's Story
Mistystar's Omen
Cloudstar's Journey
Tigerclaw's Fury
Leafpool's Wish
Dovewing's Silence

SEEKERS

SURVIVORS
STORM OF DOGS

ERIN
HUNTER

HARPER

An Imprint of HarperCollinsPublishers

Special thanks to Inbali Iserles

Storm of Dogs
Copyright © 2015 by Working Partners Limited
Series created by Working Partners Limited
Endpaper art © 2015 by Frank Riccio and Laszlo Kubinyi
All rights reserved. Printed in the United States of America.
No part of this book may be used or reproduced in any manner
whatsoever without written permission except in the case of
brief quotations embodied in critical articles and reviews.
For information address HarperCollins Children's Books,
a division of HarperCollins Publishers,
195 Broadway, New York, NY 10007.
www.harpercollinschildrens.com

Library of Congress Cataloging-in-Publication Data
Hunter, Erin.
 Storm of dogs / Erin Hunter. — First edition.
  pages cm. — (Survivors ; #6)
 Summary: "Lucky and the dogs of the Wild Pack must fight tooth and claw to survive the storm
of dogs—the terrifying battle that has been haunting Lucky's dreams"— Provided by publisher.
 ISBN 978-0-06-210276-8 (trade bdg.) — ISBN 978-0-06-210277-5 (lib. bdg.)
 [1. Dogs—Fiction. 2. Wild dogs—Fiction. 3. Survival—Fiction. 4. Adventure and adventurers—
Fiction. 5. Fantasy.] I. Title.
PZ7.H916625Sto 2015   2014022224
[Fic]—dc23   CIP
                                                                                  AC

Typography based on a design by Hilary Zarycky
15 16 17 18 19 CG/RRDH 10 9 8 7 6 5 4 3 2 1
❖
First Edition

For Noah Alexander

PACK LIST

WILD PACK (IN ORDER OF RANK)

ALPHA:

small swift-dog with short gray fur (also known as Sweet)

HUNTERS:

SNAP—small female with tan-and-white fur

LUCKY—gold-and-white thick-furred male

BRUNO—large thick-furred brown male Fight Dog with a hard face

BELLA—gold-and-white thick-furred female

MICKEY—sleek black-and-white Farm Dog

STORM—brown-and-tan female Fierce Dog

PATROL DOGS:

MOON—black-and-white female Farm Dog

DART—lean brown-and-white female chase-dog

MARTHA—giant thick-furred black female with a broad head

DAISY—small white-furred female with a brown tail

WHINE—small, black, oddly shaped dog with tiny ears and a wrinkled face

BEETLE—black-and-white shaggy-furred male (pup of Fiery and Moon)

THORN—black shaggy-furred female (pup of Fiery and Moon)

OMEGA:

small female with long white fur (also known as
Sunshine)

FIERCE DOGS (IN ORDER OF RANK)

ALPHA:

sleek black-and-brown female with a white fang-
shaped mark below her ear (also known as Blade)

BETA:

huge black-and-tan male (also known as Mace)

DAGGER—brown-and-tan male with a stubby face

PISTOL—black-and-tan female

BRUTE—black-and-tan male

RIPPER—black-and-tan female

REVOLVER—black-and-tan male

AXE—large black-and-brown male

SCYTHE—large black-and-tan female

BLUDGEON—massive black-and-tan male

MUSKET—black-and-brown male

CANNON—brown-and-tan female

LANCE—black-and-tan male

ARROW—young black-and-tan male

BULLET—smaller black-and-brown male

FANG—brown-and-tan male

OMEGA:

half wolf with gray-and-white fur and yellow eyes

TWITCH'S PACK

ALPHA:

tan chase-dog with black patches and three legs (also known as Twitch)

BETA:

small, wiry-furred black male (also known as Splash)

CHASE—small ginger-furred female

WHISPER—skinny gray male

RAKE—scrawny male with wiry fur and a scarred muzzle

WOODY—stocky brown male

BREEZE—small brown female with large ears and short fur

OMEGA:

small black female (also known as Ruff)

PROLOGUE

Lucky awoke with a start, springing to his paws. Fear prickled along his back and gathered hotly in his throat. He felt dizzy with the urge to run, but there was nowhere to go. His eyes darted to the metal bars that blocked his way.

The smell of other dogs rose on the air with their terrified yips and whimpers. Lucky shook his fur in confusion. He knew this place....

The Trap House!

How had he found himself back in here? He twisted toward the next cage, sniffing urgently for Sweet. He picked up her friendly, comforting scent, his whiskers trembling.

"Sweet? Sweet, something's on its way. Something bad."

"Yes, I feel it! What's happening?" Sweet's yelp was sharp and panicked.

Lucky threw his forepaws against the wire door, but it wouldn't budge. Whimpers rose along the wall of cages. It was just like before—they were all trapped.

"Sweet!" he barked. "It must be happening again—the Big Growl! Can you feel it?"

He could hear her shuffling, squeezing against the metal wall that separated them. "But it's over, Lucky," she whined. "It already happened. It can't happen again."

Despite the dread in her voice, the swift-dog's words reassured him. Sweet's right. The Big Growl came and we escaped. We don't need to worry this time—it's just a bad memory.

The ground began trembling, and he could hear the crack and hiss of splitting hardstone overhead. The other dogs in the Trap House started howling in panic. Their fear-scent rose in sickening waves.

Lucky barked over the howling dogs. "You're right, Sweet! It's happened before, it can't happen again!" His voice wavered with uncertainty. "Even if it does, we escaped last time—we survived."

With another crack, a billow of dust tumbled from the ceiling like snow. Lucky blinked furiously, hardly able to see.

"But something feels different this time," whimpered Sweet.

Lucky's throat tightened, and his tail shrank against his flank. The swift-dog was right. In all the times he had dreamed about the Big Growl, Lucky had known they would escape. This time—

He didn't have a chance to finish his thought. The ground began to shake violently and he lost his footing, skidding onto his side with a thump. He heard a shriek of tearing metal and shattering clear-stone. Dogs were howling in terror as the traps started tumbling and smashing against the splitting ground. Through the mist of white dust, Lucky saw one cage drive into another, crushing the dogs inside. He scrambled onto his paws, eyes wide in horror. Then his own cage started shaking and shifting.

"Lucky! Help me!" barked Sweet, her claws scratching against the door to her cage.

He pressed forward at the sound of her voice, poking his paw through the wire mesh at the front of his cage and scrabbling to get out. "I'm coming!" he assured her. But as he worked at the wire, prickles of doubt ran down his back. Part of the Trap House wall should have fallen in by now, knocking Sweet's cage to the ground and breaking it open, and ripping loose the corner of the wire from Lucky's cage. That was how they'd escaped. It was different this time. . . .

The ground was shaking harder now, and the sounds of tearing, smashing, and barking was deafening. Lucky's cage lurched forward with a sharp jerk, and another shove sent it plummeting toward the hardstone floor. It landed upside-down. A searing pain shot along Lucky's back, and he howled. I thought this was a dream! he told himself. I'm not supposed to feel pain in a dream! Was he wrong? Was this really happening?

Wincing, he clambered to his paws, preparing to escape. Chunks of debris were falling from the ceiling, raining down on the broken cage. Lucky shuffled forward and extended a forepaw, preparing to climb out.

But the door of his cage had not sprung open.

He squinted through the dust and debris till he spotted Sweet. She was furiously kicking her forepaws against the walls of her cage, close to Lucky but divided by walls of mesh and crumbling hardstone. Her dark eyes met his, and she threw back her head and howled. "This isn't how it happened! We escaped the Trap House! We're supposed to get away!"

"We did get away!" he barked back. "We will *survive!*" With a huge effort, he threw himself against the door of his cage, working furiously to force it open. He felt it creak beneath his paws with a wave of euphoria. Thank the Sky-Dogs, he uttered silently.

Then the ceiling started rumbling, and Lucky shrank back in confusion. The walls were shaking dangerously—the cage shuddered like a leaf in the wind. The air was pierced with the screech of tearing hardstone, and Lucky's whole world collapsed.

CHAPTER ONE

Lucky's eyes snapped open, and a terrified whine escaped his throat. He caught his breath, his ears pricking up. Gone were the crashes and howls of the Trap House.

It was *a dream . . . and we* did *survive!*

He breathed deeply, relief coursing through his limbs. The night air was silent and cool. From the mouth of the den he could see an icy breeze stirring the leafless branches of the trees that dotted the territory. He saw the grassy slope near the top of the cliffs, the place where he and the rescue party had found the Pack after their failed mission to save their friend, Fiery. Sweet had decided that they would stay there, despite the dangers they faced—they had expended too much energy in their endless hunt for safer territories.

Lucky turned to look at Sweet, the Pack's Alpha and his new

5

mate. The swift-dog was curled against Lucky's side, her warm body soothing against his fur as her chest rose and fell in sleep. Her cream muzzle twitched and relaxed, and she snored gently. Lucky felt his whiskers prickle with a familiar sense of affection. He licked her nose very gently. Sweet snuffled, but she didn't wake up.

Rising to his paws and stretching, Lucky peered about their den, a sort of cave built of hedges and ivy. It was the best den in the territory, once claimed by their half-wolf previous Alpha. He shuddered as he thought of the half wolf. *That traitor! Siding with Blade and the Fierce Dogs* . . .

Lucky trod out of the den onto frosty grass that crunched beneath his paws. The trees and the incline of the land blocked the worst of the wind that bounded over the Endless Lake. Still, its icy touch ruffled Lucky's fur, and he shivered. The sky was a thick, dark pelt, with tiny glinting stars like watchful eyes. Lucky picked his way between his sleeping Packmates, who were hunkered down between shrubs. Not all of them had wanted to stay in this territory upon the cliffs, so close to the deserted longpaw town below where the Fierce Dogs had made their lair. Sweet had been resolute: They could make hunting trips over the hills while prey was sparse, but the Pack was staying put. Constantly wandering would tire out every dog. They needed a base, a territory to defend—a camp to call home.

No dog had challenged her authority.

Lucky had wanted to stay too . . . but he had other reasons for believing that they had to make a stand.

As Lucky crept between the dogs, his eyes rested on Storm. Her sleeping body twitched with tension and her top lip sprang up, revealing a long white fang. Muscles clenched beneath her fur—even in sleep, she looked ferocious. Lucky paused, his ears twisting back, wondering what she was dreaming about to make her so tense. It couldn't be the Big Growl—she hadn't even been alive when it had happened.

A low snarl escaped Storm's lips, and Lucky shifted uneasily from paw to paw. Was she reliving her brutal fight with her litter-brother Fang? Nearly a full journey of the Moon-Dog had passed since the fight, and Storm's ugly purple scars had almost healed. The Fierce Dogs' Trial of Rage demanded that one dog kill the other, but they had both survived—Storm had proven her maturity and self-control, sparing her brother despite his frenzied attack. Remembering the young dog's loyalty and resilience, Lucky's chest swelled with pride.

With a sudden jerk, Storm sprang onto her paws, her eyes wide open, her gaze darting back and forth in the darkness as though she expected an enemy to be there. Then they rested on Lucky and she sat back down, her tail wagging gently.

He padded toward her and touched her nose with his. "How are you feeling?"

Storm flexed her forepaw. "Much better. Look! It doesn't hurt anymore when I put weight on it!" She demonstrated, trotting a circle around Lucky.

Lucky inspected her face. The scratches around her muzzle had healed well, but the missing scrap of her left ear would never grow back. He glanced at the dogs sleeping nearby. "Let's step away from the den."

The young Fierce Dog nodded and followed him to the first of the low trees that led to the pond. "What are you doing up before the Sun-Dog?" she asked.

Lucky sighed. Telling Storm about his dreams would only alarm her. "As the Ice Wind deepens, the Sun-Dog sleeps longer. But we dogs don't have such a luxury." He turned his head away and sniffed the air, trying to hide it from Storm—he thought he could smell the sharp scent of snow.

"The longer we sleep, the more vulnerable we are to attack," Storm agreed. She paused, tilting her dark head. "But perhaps the prey-creatures are also sleeping longer. Maybe we can have an easy hunt!"

Lucky wagged his tail encouragingly. "We can try." He felt the need to be out there, searching between the trees and tracking the territory to the cliffs. The Patrol Dogs kept watch over their territory both night and day, and there'd been no sign of their enemies since the battle between Storm and Fang. But Lucky knew the Wild Dogs couldn't rest. While Blade and the attack-dogs were out there, his Pack would always be in danger.

The Sun-Dog was flexing his whiskers above the horizon when Storm appeared at Lucky's side. She dropped a large, plump bird, its pale, tawny feathers tipped with gray, by the one that Lucky had already caught. The birds' necks were long and black and their faces were black too, except for thick white marks beneath their beaks. Over the past days, Lucky had seen giant Packs of these birds soaring overhead, flying across the Endless Lake. They all appeared from the same direction, each Pack following their own Alphas.

How do they all know where to go? Lucky wondered, not for the first time. Could the birds sense things that dogs could not, like the direction of warm skies? Did they follow the Sun-Dog to lands where he never fell asleep and it was always bright?

Several of the birds had gathered on the rocks near the cliffs. That was how Lucky and Storm had made their kills—high in the sky, the birds were graceful and fast, but on the rocks they shuffled awkwardly.

Lucky and Storm picked up the prey-creatures and made their way back to the camp. The other dogs were awake, stretching in the low light of sunup while Daisy, who had watched over the Pack as they slept, napped in the Patrol Dogs' den. She lifted her head and the other dogs yipped excitedly as Lucky and Storm approached.

Beetle ran loops around the returning dogs, licking his chops. He was joined by his litter-sister, Thorn, who bounded up to the birds and sniffed them uncertainly.

"What *are* they?" She prodded one with an outstretched paw. "I've never seen such a long neck!"

Beetle's eyes widened, and he paused. "Only Lucky could catch such strange creatures!" he yelped, awestruck. "The Spirit Dogs are on your side!"

Lucky wasn't sure what sort of birds they were, but before he could answer, Moon padded next to her pups. "They're geese," she commented with a wry twitch of her pointed black ears.

Knowing the creatures' name did nothing to dampen Beetle's enthusiasm. "Lucky, do you think your Father-Dog could have been a Spirit Dog?" he barked.

Sweet emerged from the den and met Lucky's eye, her head cocked in amusement.

She's laughing at me—at Beetle's hero worship.

"No," Lucky said quickly, embarrassed. "I'm sure he wasn't, Beetle."

Lucky looked back at the pup. He was a little smaller than his litter-sister. Like their Mother-Dog, Moon, his fur was black and white, but his snout was stubby and his limbs were broad. *He's looking more like Fiery every day. And I guess he's trying to find someone to replace his Father-Dog.*

After the dogs had shared the geese, taking turns by rank from Sweet down to Sunshine, the Pack Omega, some of them gathered for a fight-training session with Storm. The young Fierce Dog demonstrated how to dodge and block blows as the others watched.

"The trick is speed," she told them. "Your opponent won't see you coming. Your aim is to get the advantage, push them to the ground, and hold them by the throat."

Lucky looked to the assembled dogs, nervously gauging their reactions. Mickey and Snap were doing their best to mimic Storm's forward dip, outstretching their forepaws. Bruno jutted out his paw with a stiff grunt as Bella and Martha took turns practicing the blocking. Even Whine, usually the first to complain about fight-training, was watching with interest. Lucky gave an inward sigh of relief. None of the dogs seemed to mind taking instructions from Storm, regardless of rank.

It's good for everyone that the rules are more relaxed than they were under the half wolf. Storm has skills that she can share; it would be foolish to let rank get in the way. Working together . . . that's what a Pack's all about.

"Daisy, can I demonstrate the move on you?" asked Storm. "It won't hurt."

The wiry-furred white dog gave an excited yip of agreement and stood at attention. Storm jabbed at her with fangs exposed. When Daisy moved to block the Fierce Dog, Storm dived down, dodging Daisy's teeth and seizing the small dog by her neck. For a moment, she pinned Daisy to the ground. Then she sprang back and Daisy rolled onto her paws.

Storm gave her a friendly lick and turned to the others. "Now you try it."

"It's harder for me," whined Thorn. "My muzzle isn't as big as yours. Even when I'm fully grown, I'll never be able to close my jaws around another dog's neck."

Storm barked insistently, "Any dog can do this move, even smaller ones. It's not about size, it's about confidence. It doesn't matter if you don't have the best hold. An enemy—*any enemy*—will panic when he feels fangs at his throat."

Lucky didn't doubt that this was true, but he wondered how Storm knew it. And where had she learned the dive-and-block technique? She had been raised by the Wild Pack, not the Fierce Dogs. She had never been *taught* these deadly moves.

She must know how to fight instinctively.

He was glad that the traitorous half wolf wasn't here to see this. The old Alpha had never trusted Storm. Lucky's tail dropped a little at the thought, and he watched as Beetle took his position in front of Thorn. The pup's dark muzzle quivered, and he took a step back. *He's scared that his litter-sister is going to rip his throat out!* Lucky realized. Was the exercise too tough for the young dogs?

Thorn sprang at him, jabbing with her teeth, as Storm had, before diving down to Beetle's throat. The young dog moved quickly, yipping in triumph, but her litter-brother shook and freed himself, tipping her off balance. Thorn rolled onto her side, and Beetle threw his forepaws on her flank, pinning her down.

Then he glanced nervously at Storm. "I'm sorry . . . that wasn't supposed to happen, I just . . ." He dropped back, head lowered, as his litter-sister rose to her paws with an apologetic whine.

A ripple of apprehension ran down Lucky's back. Moon's pups were only a little younger than Storm, yet they cowered before her. *Is it something Storm's doing—some kind of natural dominance?*

The young Fierce Dog gave Thorn a little nudge. "Don't worry, you're learning—it takes practice to get it right." She turned to Beetle. "And you shouldn't feel bad for having good instincts— they could save you in a fight."

Lucky's tension drained away, and his tail rose with a relieved wag. *Storm isn't the angry attack-dog that Alpha took her for. She's showing patience and understanding. She's more like us than the Fierce Dogs.*

Feeling a wave of pride, Lucky turned and started padding between the trees. Storm didn't need him standing over her. *I trust her.* His paws crunched over the frosty grass as he made his way to the edge of the camp where the cliffs hung over the Endless Lake. The air was salty and so cold that it cut beneath Lucky's fur. Gray clouds gathered in the sky, bringing with them the promise of harsher weather. He closed his eyes, remembering the swirling snow he had seen in the dreams he used to have: the dreams about the Storm of Dogs. When he opened them, he thought he saw a flash of dark fur slip between the trees.

Lucky's breath caught in his throat. He blinked, peering at the trees. Had he imagined it? He trod stealthily over the frost, doing his best to stay quiet. There was no scent on the air, and no paw prints were etched in the hard ground. He examined the circle of trees, his muzzle low. There was no sign of an unfamiliar dog, but Lucky knew he'd seen someone. His hackles rose as his eyes traced the horizon.

Was some dog here, spying on me?

Rising from the valley, Lucky could hear the yaps of the Wild Pack—they must have finished their training session. It was strange and unsettling to hear them sounding so cheerful and at ease when tension was skittering through Lucky's belly like ants. With a last glance over his shoulder, he turned tail and made his way back to the camp.

CHAPTER TWO

By the time Lucky was past the pond and hurrying toward the clearing near the rear of the camp, the Sun-Dog was high in the sky, bounding over the low trees and brushing away the clouds with his golden tail. The air that drifted under him was bitterly cold, and Lucky gazed up a moment, confused. *Why does the Sun-Dog's heat feel so far away during Ice Wind?*

He remembered the dark flash of fur that he thought he'd seen between the trees, and his pace quickened. It was probably nothing to worry about, but Sweet needed to know.

As Lucky arrived in the clearing, he was surprised to find the Pack gathered in an anxious circle. Sweet gave a sharp bark when she saw him and lifted her muzzle in reproach. "Where have you been?"

Lucky dipped his head, giving her a conciliatory lick on the nose. "I went for a walk." He was about to mention the dark-furred dog he'd spotted when Sweet cut in.

"Dart and Moon have just come back from a patrol, and they've seen something . . . *strange*."

Moon stepped forward, her blue eyes sharp. "We were patrolling the perimeter of the town down by the Endless Lake."

Lucky flexed his whiskers. "Just the two of you? You shouldn't go there without a bigger patrol—you know that's where the Fierce Dogs have made their camp."

The Farm Dog raised her white muzzle. "That's just it. We didn't smell any Fierce Dogs."

"It's like they just *vanished*," Dart put in. The skinny brown-and-white chase-dog paced nervously next to Moon, gazing beyond the trees to the distant cliffs.

"But we did hear something else," growled Moon, her lip peeling back. Her long ears flattened in agitation, and Lucky grew wary. "*Longpaws*," she spat. "Just when we thought we were rid of them."

Bella and Mickey took a step closer, and the Pack exchanged worried looks.

Moon turned to Sweet. "It sounded like there were a lot of them, and we thought we should check it out with our Alpha before going any closer."

Bella cocked her head, puzzled. "Do you mean to say that the longpaws have returned, after all this time?"

Looking back toward the cliffs, Lucky was thoughtful. The longpaws had been gone so long, and so much had changed. He remembered treading the streets of the city, begging for a meal at the Food House and sleeping in the park. But that was a lifetime ago, before the Big Growl.

Sunshine scrambled between Bruno and Martha, her filthy tail giving a cheerful wag. "The longpaws? Back in their cities and towns?"

Sweet frowned. "Surely the important question is, what *sort* of longpaws? Are these the nasty, yellow-pelted creatures that captured Fiery?"

Moon growled, her hackles rising. "We weren't close enough to see them, but if those yellow longpaws have *dared* to come back, I'll get rid of them!"

Beetle and Thorn yipped their agreement, making a show of snarling and bounding in circles.

"Let's get them!" growled Thorn, throwing down her black-and-white forepaws.

Lucky rose to his paws. "Before we do anything, we need to see what the longpaws are doing. It will be no-sun soon enough."

"We're not going anywhere tonight," said Sweet with a firm look. "The Sun-Dog's journeys are short during Ice Wind—he's already high overhead and he'll soon run for his den. I don't want us traveling during no-sun; it's dangerous. In the morning I will lead a larger patrol, and we'll find out what the longpaws are up to. Lucky, I want you by my side. Also Bella, Moon, Mickey, Martha, and . . ." She surveyed the gathered dogs. "Omega." Her eyes rested on Sunshine.

The dirty white long-haired dog yipped in surprise, her eyes round. "You want *me*?"

"You have experience with different types of longpaws, and that could be valuable."

Sunshine's tail wagged furiously. Lucky turned to his mate. He was glad that under Sweet's leadership, the dogs' talents were more important than where they fit in the Pack ranks. Sunshine had been overlooked so many times, and he knew it meant a lot to her to be able to contribute.

His thoughts were interrupted by Storm, who had sidled up to Sweet. "I should come too," insisted the Fierce Dog. "Just in case anything goes wrong. I'm a good fighter."

Lucky stiffened. The last thing they needed was a confrontation, and if Blade's Pack was still in the town after all, it would be dangerous to have Storm with them. They might seek revenge against Storm for beating Fang in the Trial of Rage, or challenge her to another trial. "It's important that you stay here," he said quickly. "With so many of us in the town, who will defend the camp? You're strong and brave, and we need you to look out for the others."

Standing beside the young Fierce Dog, Sweet gave Lucky a grateful look. He knew she didn't want Storm in the town any more than he did.

Storm snorted. She didn't seem particularly thrilled at the prospect of staying behind, but Lucky's praise had reassured her. "Okay," she replied. "I'll make sure the camp is safe."

The next morning at sunup, Sweet led the patrol along the rugged cliff path toward the Endless Lake. Lucky peered at the lashing waves as they rolled over the sand far below, breaking in bursts of mist. The cold expanse of water still scared him, but he was used to it now. As the dogs hopped down the rock crags toward the bank, he noticed that the water smelled less salty than it had when the air was warmer.

The path became narrow, and Lucky fell back behind Sweet. He glanced over his shoulder to see Mickey, Bella, and Moon.

Martha was walking slowly, helping Sunshine over the steeper rocks.

The route down the cliff took them alongside a small stream. Lucky paused to drink but hesitated. The water looked different. He stepped closer, his paws crunching on the frosty grass. He prodded the edge of the water with his paw. It tingled with cold. *Ice* . . . well, more a sort of sludgy half ice. But he could see that the water was growing harder, just like . . . Lucky's ears flicked back.

Like a dog's body after death.

He had seen puddles freeze in the city, but could that happen to the mighty River-Dog? Was the Spirit Dog sick? Lucky's eyes darted over the narrow path of the stream, which gleamed pale blue, frozen still. It must have been so cold for the River-Dog; she couldn't escape over the horizon like the Sun-Dog. Lucky whimpered, his tail drifting to his flank. He tried not to think about the River-Dog as he followed Sweet down the last of the rocks onto the high bank of the Endless Lake. They prowled along the edges of the town.

Sweet turned to Lucky. "I can hardly smell the Fierce Dogs."

It was true—their scent was very faint. They must have abandoned their camp in the longpaw building. But where had they gone?

As the patrol drew closer to the town, Lucky could hear the barks of longpaws. Then he caught a low, familiar grumble. *Loudcages!* Moon whimpered quietly, and her tail drooped.

Sweet paused, then addressed the dogs. "There certainly seem to be a lot of longpaws around. I want to try to work out what they're up to and if they're here to stay, so we'll have to get nearer. Follow me and be very careful. Walk in a line, close to the wall. That way we won't be so easy to spot." She started stalking along the edge of a building, and Lucky followed at a distance. Glancing back over his shoulder, he saw his litter-sister Bella creeping after him, shrinking against the hardstone wall. She tipped her head at him, and her eyes glittered with excitement.

The barking of longpaws and the roar of loudcages grew louder.

When she reached the end of the street, Sweet crouched down and peered around the corner. Her tail fell between her legs and Lucky couldn't resist creeping up alongside her to get a better view of what she was seeing.

He was shocked to see a large number of longpaws pacing up and down the next street, calling to each other. Their pelts were orange, not yellow, and their heads were covered with shiny, hard shells. There was sand and rubble everywhere, and several of the longpaws were sweeping up some of it into neat mounds. Two others climbed into a huge yellow loudcage with a single, enormous tooth. It rumbled to life, dragging its tooth along the ground and picking up large chunks of debris.

Sweet and Lucky retreated, joining the other dogs in the shelter of a doorway. The swift-dog told them what she and Lucky had seen.

Moon was thoughtful. "They don't sound like the same longpaws who killed Fiery. And it does seem like the Fierce Dogs have gone."

Bella licked her chops. "It may be worth sticking around to find out if there's anything worth stealing. Where there are longpaws, there is usually food."

Moon looked uncertain. "Longpaws are dangerous."

"They aren't all bad!" whined Mickey. He dropped his muzzle defensively, and Lucky felt a familiar tightness in his belly. The Farm Dog had made so much progress since the Big Growl. Of all the Leashed Dogs, he had found it hardest to give up the hope that his longpaws were coming back. It would be a disaster if after all this time, Mickey started pining for his old life again.

But it was Sunshine who broke forward with a volley of excited yips, running onto the street. "I want to see them!"

Lucky went to block her, but Mickey got there first. Martha sprang forward to help him, placing a large, webbed paw in front of the excited Omega. "No, not yet," she soothed in her deep, gentle voice. "We don't know if they're friendly."

The little dog faltered. "I'm sorry," she whined. "You're right . . . I don't know what got into me."

"Oh no!" Bella howled, aiming a worried look at Sunshine. "Now look what you've done!"

A couple of the longpaws had heard the commotion and were pointing at the dogs. One started to approach them with cautious steps.

Lucky looked to Sweet. "What should we do? They don't *seem* aggressive."

Sweet's hackles were raised. "We don't know what they're like, and I'm not going to risk some of my best fighters. Everyone, back to camp!"

The dogs obeyed immediately, following Sweet as she hurried away from the town, scampering over the hardstone where it collapsed into sand and onto the high bank of the Endless Lake. Lucky hung back, preparing to stop Sunshine if she tried to make a break for the longpaws. But the Omega seemed to have learned her lesson. She ran by Bella's side, her little legs powering to keep up, her tail a tangle of fur behind her. Like the other dogs, she didn't look back.

Once they were up on the cliff path, hidden from the town behind curving boulders and knotted thorns, Sweet came to a stop. The other dogs gathered around her. Sunshine flopped on the ground, panting quickly—the climb was hardest on her.

Mickey turned on the little dog angrily. "By the Sky-Dogs, what were you thinking? You could have gotten us in serious trouble!"

Sunshine sighed, her head sinking onto the ground in front of her. "I know, I'm sorry. I just couldn't help myself. The moment I knew that longpaws were close, I felt a *need* to go to them. I was raised by longpaws; it's like an instinct, the need to be near them. But it has passed now."

Mickey lowered his head, his jaw softening. "I understand."

Sweet didn't look so forgiving. Lucky tensed as she approached the Omega. He hoped Sweet would be more forgiving than the half wolf had been, but the pressures of leadership could change a dog's character.

"You need to learn better self-control," she told Sunshine sternly. "We have to be able to rely on one another." She turned back toward the camp and started to retrace the route up the cliffs. Mickey and Moon followed her lead.

Sunshine rose to her paws, her head lowered solemnly, and padded after them in silence. Lucky let out his breath. Sweet hadn't changed. He should have trusted that her fair nature would hold. He felt pride and affection swell within him.

The dogs walked along the rocks. Lucky slowed his pace, drifting to the back of the group, where Sunshine was already struggling to keep up. Bella paused to walk alongside them.

Sunshine raised her head a moment to look at the littermates. "I know what you're going to say," she whined pitifully. "I wasn't actually expecting to see *my* longpaws in the group, it's just . . . I was excited to know that some had survived the Big Growl, and that they had come back. I know the yellow-furred ones are mean, but I don't hate all longpaws. Mine were always kind to me."

Lucky gave the little dog a friendly lick. "I'm not angry, Sunshine. I know you mean it when you say you want to do better. That's what counts."

He caught Bella's eye and beckoned to her with a tilt of the muzzle. The two littermates slipped away from the others, standing in a dip between rocks so they couldn't be overheard.

Bella cocked her golden head. "Is everything okay?"

"Yes, it's just . . . I was wondering. If things went back to how they were before the Big Growl—if lots of longpaws returned and set up new camps—would you want to go and live with them again?"

Bella fell silent, gnawing a bur stuck to her flank. She pulled it free and dropped it on the frosty ground. "No," she started slowly. "I can't say that I would. If my *own* longpaws returned, well, that would be different. I'm not sure I could ever turn my back on them, if they wanted me. But I'm a Pack Dog now. I've heard my dog-spirit and have gotten used to the freedom of being able to roam where I like."

Lucky's tail wagged with pride at his litter-sister's words. She was a true Wild Dog now, just like him. With the dog-wolf gone, it felt as though the Pack was finally working together for a common goal—survival.

CHAPTER THREE

The frost had melted on the ragged grass of the camp, but Lucky still shivered in the bitter air. The afternoon was tinged with a violet light. Sweet lifted her long, pale muzzle, glancing for a moment behind her, in the direction of the cliffs and the Endless Lake. Then she turned back to the Pack.

"So we left the town immediately," she finished.

Dart's eyes grew wide, and she pawed the ground. "But the longpaws saw you? They know we're here?"

Bruno gave a low growl and Snap stiffened, the fur bristling on her wiry muzzle.

Lucky looked to Sweet, admiring her calm authority.

"They saw us in the town, yes," she replied. "But they didn't follow us when we left, so they don't know the location of the camp."

Moon's blue eyes were as cool and clear as the water of the frozen stream. "In my opinion, they're still too close. We're not safe here. Those creatures hurt Fiery. If they can bring down such a powerful dog, they can do it to any one of us. What if they decide the town isn't big enough for them and they come this way?"

Dart yapped in agreement, her slim tail clinging to her flank.

Martha shook her dark head. "I don't think they'd do that," she said reasonably. "There are no longpaw houses up here for them to shelter in. They feel the cold more than we do; they'd need to have somewhere."

"That doesn't mean anything," said Mickey. "I've seen longpaws *building* their houses. There's nothing to stop them from coming here and starting to build. They're *very* clever, they can do anything, and . . ." He trailed off, looking guilty. "I'm not saying they're good, I don't mean . . ."

He doesn't want the other dogs to think he's still loyal to the longpaws, thought Lucky. He gave the Farm Dog a reassuring look, then turned back to Sweet. The Pack watched her expectantly.

Sweet spoke decisively. "I'm not scared of longpaws. We're better hunters than them, and by Tree Flower there will be plenty of prey in the surrounding valleys. Till then, we'll make do with geese and whatever else we can catch."

"What about the Fierce Dogs?" whined Dart. "What if they come back to the town? Where *are* they?"

Sweet raised her muzzle. "The Pack isn't going to move again. I'm sick of running away. It will just tire us out and leave us unable to fight—and we may have to yet." Her tail jerked and her eyes flashed. "If the Fierce Dogs come back, we'll deal with them." She looked at Martha and Mickey. "If the longpaws want the town, they can have it. But the cliffs and the valley belong to us."

"What if the longpaws come here?" whined Dart. "Mickey said—"

"We're not going *anywhere*," snapped Sweet.

Silenced, the skinny chase-dog lowered her head. A tangible sense of relief ran through the Pack. Few had the appetite to move again, particularly during Ice Wind.

When Sweet spoke again, her tone was softer. "There will be a ceremony tomorrow, when the Sun-Dog begins his next journey."

Lucky cocked his head. "What kind of ceremony? All the dogs have names. . . ."

Sweet met his eye. "A ceremony to mark your role as my Pack's Beta."

The original members of the Wild Pack barked in excitement, and Lucky felt his fur tingle.

Snap's tail was wagging as she turned to the perplexed former Leashed Dogs. "Every dog except the Beta needs to find something they can offer to the Spirit Dogs."

"It could be the pelt of a prey-creature," said Moon, "or maybe a feather, or a special pebble. Something to show the Spirit Dogs we are keeping them in our thoughts, and to represent the qualities we wish for in our Beta."

"I saw some pretty white stones by the pond," yipped Sunshine. "They shone with the light of the Moon-Dog. Will they do?"

Moon's ears flicked back with satisfaction. "They will do very well."

The Pack dispersed to hunt for offerings, leaving Lucky alone in the grassy clearing. He hadn't been around when Sweet was made the half wolf's Beta, and he had no idea what to expect.

I used to be a Lone Dog, responsible for nothing, looking after no dog but myself.

He belonged with this Pack now, and he felt a warm, comfortable certainty about his place at Sweet's side. But could he really have gone from a Lone Dog to a high-ranking Pack Dog in such a short time?

Am I really ready for this?

* * *

As the sky darkened, Lucky padded over to the den he shared with Sweet. The swift-dog was out with the others, searching for offerings for the Spirit Dogs. Lucky settled onto the bedding of moss and leaves with a long yawn.

Bella appeared at the entrance to the den, panting with amusement. "All the stress about the ceremony tiring you out, Yap?"

Lucky's fur bristled with irritation. "The ceremony doesn't bother me," he said gruffly. "It's the responsibility that comes with being Beta."

Bella sat on the bedding with a snort. "You're practically Sweet's Beta already—nothing will change after the ceremony. Anyway, it's the perfect role for you." There was a playful glint in her eye.

"What do you mean by that?"

"Well, this way you get to tell the other dogs what to do, without being the one who every dog looks to for answers." She leaned over and nudged him affectionately.

"What nonsense!" yapped Lucky, nipping his litter-sister's ear. She gave him a good-natured lick, and he relaxed against the bedding, panting.

Bella's face became more serious. "I've been watching Sweet

grow into her role. I know I challenged her for it, but I have to admit she makes a good Alpha, and the two of you make a good team. Having both of you in charge has given the Pack a lot of confidence—the dogs are happier than they used to be. So why not make it official?"

Lucky looked at her gratefully, feeling truly close to her for the first time since they'd joined the Wild Pack.

After Bella left to find her offering, Lucky nestled down and went to sleep. His dreams were peaceful. He saw a long, murmuring stream winding through a valley. The light was golden and the air was warm. Small flowers dotted the grassy bank, and the branches of a tree shifted in the wind, one low-hanging branch tapping him on the flank. The wind picked up and the tapping grew more insistent. No. That wasn't tapping. It felt like . . . a muzzle.

Lucky's eyes snapped open. Sweet was butting his ribs with her wet nose. The light of the Moon-Dog was weak inside the den, and he could barely see her.

"Finally!" Sweet drew back her head. "I've been trying to wake you for ages!"

Lucky rolled onto his paws, shaking away his sleepiness. "What's wrong? Is there trouble?"

Sweet shook her head. "The camp is safe. I need you to follow me quietly."

The two dogs stepped out of the den and crept around their sleeping Packmates. Moon sat with her back to them at the edge of camp, watching for danger. Mickey and Snap were curled up beneath a low bush, and a short distance away old Bruno was stretched out by himself, snoring loudly. A twig snapped under Lucky's paw, and Bruno's lip twitched but he didn't wake up.

Lucky watched Sweet's long legs step lightly over the cool grass as they left the camp for the circle of trees. He wanted to ask her what they were doing, but somehow he knew not to. She was walking with purpose, kicking aside foliage. *I guess I'll find out what's going on soon enough.*

When they reached the pond between the trees, Sweet finally stopped. The air was damp and smelled of the Earth-Dog, as it did after heavy rain, but the sky was cloudless and illuminated with a silvery light. The Moon-Dog flicked her tail over the surface of the pond and the water shimmered, rippling slowly. Would it also turn to ice, just as the stream had grown cold and hard?

Sweet stood gazing into the water, and Lucky joined her. Their reflections appeared faintly on the surface.

The swift-dog spoke without taking her eyes off the pond.

"There is a part of the ceremony that is only between an Alpha and her Beta, a part that no other dog can know about. I did it when I became Beta, and now it's your turn. You have to swear loyalty to me and vow to serve the Pack as best you can—you must do this before the Sun-Dog returns. If you do, you will begin the new day as my official Beta. Unless . . ." Her head dipped, and her eyes were hooded. She continued in a quiet voice. "Unless you'd rather not be my Beta? It isn't too late to change your mind."

Lucky reached over and licked her ear. "I don't want to change my mind."

She looked up at him. "It's just . . . you're hard to figure out sometimes. You can be the bravest dog I've ever seen, but you don't seem to want responsibility. I still remember what you said when we escaped the Trap House, all that stuff about being a Lone Dog."

"That was a lifetime ago, Sweet. I've changed." He eased himself down onto his haunches. "Before the Big Growl, I had only myself to answer to, only myself to look after, and I was fine with that. When I met Bella and the Leashed Dogs, all of them looked to me to make decisions, and I started to dread the day when I ran out of answers—when I let them down." He cleared his throat with a gruff cough. "Some Lone Dog I turned out to be!"

Sweet rested her head against his neck. Her voice was soft. "Haven't you learned yet? You were *never* a Lone Dog, not really— you just hadn't found your Pack yet. You've proven that you want to serve the Pack to the best of your ability. The only question now is, will you be loyal to me, whatever happens?"

Lucky tried to shift his position so he could look her in the eye, but Sweet's head was heavy on his neck. Instead he spoke into the darkness. "*Always.* You should know that by now. Whatever happens, I will always stand by you."

Sweet gave a satisfied sigh. "Thank you, Lucky. I needed to hear that."

Then she plunged her fangs into his neck.

CHAPTER FOUR

Searing pain shot through Lucky. Sweet bit harder, forcing her teeth deeper into his flesh. A choked whine escaped Lucky's throat, but he was too shocked to move.

She's attacking me!

Sweet lowered her chest against his back, her thin tail curving around Lucky's flank. He froze beneath her weight, feeling the pressure of her chest as it expanded and relaxed with each breath. His limbs tingled, and he struggled to order his thoughts. Pain surged through the deep punctures in his skin, and his pulse thumped against his ribs. Or was it Sweet's pulse? They seemed to be thumping to the same beat.

Feeling flooded back to Lucky's limbs as Sweet eased her grip. His leg muscles flexed. He could throw her off now, turn on her angrily, but he found he didn't *want* to. His body relaxed beneath

Sweet's grip. He hardly noticed the pain in his neck as her warm, soft pelt pressed against his. It felt right to be so close to her. *This is where I'm meant to be.*

He felt Sweet's breathing slow down to the same pace as his. Then she let go of his neck and slipped off his back, stepping around him to meet him face-on.

Lucky stared at her, seeing his own blood glistening on her fangs. It dribbled down her bottom lip and spilled onto the grass. "I have bitten you beneath your fur," Sweet said solemnly. "It is a mark that no other dog will ever see. But the wound will scar, and *we* will know it is there. You are my Beta, and you must always be loyal to me."

Lucky's tail drooped, and he dipped his head. His body seemed to know what to do, and the right words seemed to slip from his tongue. "We will know," he echoed. "I bear your mark, and I will always be loyal to you, Sweet—my Alpha."

A ripple of unease ran over his fur. *Alpha . . .*

Had Sweet gone through the same ritual, when *she* became the Pack's Beta . . . when she had sworn her loyalty to the half wolf? Lucky's eyes trailed over Sweet's long neck. The short fur looked smooth and velvety in the light of the Moon-Dog. But was there a mark underneath it, a sign that no other dog could see—that only

Sweet and the Pack's former leader knew about?

Jealousy pricked at Lucky's whiskers. He could hardly stand to think of his mate so close to the dog-wolf.

Sweet gazed at him unblinking. "You have accepted your role as my Beta. In turn, as your Alpha, I promise by the Moon-Dog to always be honorable, honest, and courageous. I will reward your loyalty by always protecting you." She lowered her muzzle but held his gaze. "If I ever break this promise, or I'm no longer Alpha, the connection between us will be broken. And if it is broken because I do something wrong—because I fail you as your Alpha—it can never be repaired." Lucky caught a glimmer of anger in Sweet's brown eyes. Was she thinking of the dog-wolf's treachery?

He took a step toward her and she licked his nose, her eyes softening.

"Now the secret ritual is over," she murmured. "With the Moon-Dog as our witness, we are bound together, and together we will lead the Pack."

Sweet and Lucky padded back to their den and curled up alongside each other. In moments, the swift-dog was fast asleep, her head resting against Lucky's side. But Lucky couldn't sleep. He wondered at the strange events that had brought him here—and his dark dreams, which warned of change to come.

It seemed an age till the Sun-Dog stretched under a heavy gray sky and Sweet opened her eyes. "How's your neck?"

Lucky blinked at her, realizing to his surprise that he could hardly feel the bite. "It's fine," he murmured.

"Good. It's time for the formal ritual." She licked his ears and led him out of the den.

This time the rest of the Pack joined them in the clearing before the trees. They formed a loose circle around Lucky, placing their individual offerings between their forepaws.

Lucky looked from the reassuring face of Martha to Daisy, Snap, Dart, and Storm. His eyes trailed across the rest of the Pack, over to Moon and her pups. He shifted from paw to paw, feeling strange. He wasn't used to rituals beneath the light of the Sun-Dog, and he felt awkward sitting alone with his Packmates staring at him.

Standing between Bella and Mickey, Sweet raised her muzzle. "My chosen Beta stands before the Pack. Make your offerings."

Bright-eyed Snap was the first to step forward. She placed her gift in front of Lucky—the bones of a small creature, recently caught and killed. Small lumps of red gristle still clung to the curving ribs. Lucky sniffed the offering, then looked up at Snap.

As their eyes met, she spoke solemnly.

"I bring you this gift so that you will lead successful hunts and make sure that the Pack never goes hungry." She reached forward to touch his nose, then stepped back to rejoin the ring of dogs.

Martha was the next to step into the circle. She laid a bright-yellow stone in front of him. He recognized it as one of the pebbles from the bank of the pond. She had probably gone to collect it with Sunshine, who was proudly clutching a white water stone in her mouth. "This stone was particularly clear and smooth," said the great black dog in her deep, gentle voice. "I bring you this gift so that, as the River-Dog softens the hard edges of the bank, you will smooth over the cracks and divisions in the Pack to keep us working as one." She touched his nose, and he closed his eyes. There was something so warm and reassuring about her company. For a moment, Lucky remembered his Mother-Dog.

My dear pup, the world outside may feel large and dangerous. But whatever happens, the Spirit Dogs will be watching over you. When you call for them, they will come—they will protect you.

When Lucky opened his eyes, Martha had retreated to the circle and Bruno was stepping forward. The gruff old dog dropped a sturdy branch on the ground before Lucky. He kept his head low as he spoke. "The branch is strong. It represents your courage and honor. No wind or rain can ever break it."

Lucky's fur tingled, and he gazed at Bruno. *He won't meet my eye. He still feels bad about siding with the dog-wolf when he wanted me out of the Pack.* It was Lucky who reached over and touched Bruno's nose, silently vowing to let the old brown dog understand that he could stop feeling bad about the past—it had long been forgotten.

Soon every dog had made an offering and explained its symbolism. The Pack stood in a respectful silence, most eyes on Lucky—their new Beta. Only Storm did not look at him. Instead she gazed up at the sky.

Lucky padded up to her. "Is something wrong?" he murmured.

"Not 'wrong,' but . . ." She cocked her head, still looking up. "Have you noticed how the Sun-Dog runs from one side of the sky to the other? He makes the same journey every day, always in the same direction. How does he get back to the start of his journey without us seeing him?"

Lucky frowned. He had never thought of that before. "I don't know," he admitted.

Storm lowered her eyes. "You don't?"

Lucky was sorry to disappoint her, but Storm wasn't a pup anymore—she had to learn. *She wants me to give her all the answers. But sometimes, there are no answers.*

He was startled by Sweet giving a piercing howl. He saw his mate's face aimed toward the sky, her neck fur bristling as the sound surged from her throat. After a long howl, she brought her head down, letting her eyes rove over each and every dog.

"The ceremony is over," she said, "and my Beta is confirmed. Tomorrow the Pack will be stronger than ever."

She threw her head back to howl again. This time, every dog howled with her.

That night as Lucky lay beside Sweet in their den, he felt closer to her than ever. It was official now—they weren't only mates, they were Alpha and Beta. He sighed as he closed his eyes and felt the rise and fall of Sweet's flank against his. *If only I'd known what the future held when we first met in the Trap House. I wouldn't have waited till the Big Growl! I'd have gnawed my way through to her cage and told her that we'd be okay.*

He closed his eyes, lingering on this thought. He pictured the wire bars of the cages. He could almost smell the dogs imprisoned in rows and the fear-scent rising off their fur.

Lucky turned to Sweet, but cold lengths of wire had appeared between them, and he could no longer reach the swift-dog. The air hissed with danger, and Lucky's tail shrank against his leg. He sniffed urgently, sensing sleeping dogs in neighboring cages. Something deadly was coming, but it had no shape, no scent. . . .

Lucky sprang to his paws with a startled whine, just as the ground started shaking beneath his paws. The Big Growl! But it's already happened! *Lucky howled.* The Big Growl destroyed the city, but we survived! Why do I keep coming back to the Trap House? What does it mean?

On the other side of the bars, Sweet was still asleep. Lucky had opened his mouth to bark when he saw a small, plump dog hurrying along the corridor. Intrigued, Lucky cocked his head to look, pressing his paw against the wire door to his cage. The door faded in front of him, and Lucky scrambled out onto the ground. As he turned to look around the Trap House, the wire cages disappeared before his eyes.

Lucky gasped in amazement. Shivering, he glanced down at his paws. The ground beneath him had turned to ice. What was happening?

He looked up into a dark, freezing world. Mist hung over the horizon, like a pelt on the sky. The thickset dog emerged from the gloom. The fur along his back was dark, but his forepaws were white. Lucky gave a startled bark.

Alfie!

The Leashed Dog turned to Lucky, bright-eyed. He carried no wounds from his fight with the Wild Pack's former Alpha. It was almost as though he had never been hurt.

"You're alive!" *Lucky barked, running to his old friend.*

Alfie took a step back and shook his head slowly.

Lucky froze in his steps. He could see now that the outline of Alfie's body blurred against the sky, just like the clouds. Then Lucky understood.

This isn't the waking world. . . .

"Why am I dreaming of you?" he asked.

"Because everything changed when I died," Alfie replied. "After my death, every dog was set walking along a new path, and yours has brought you here."

"Here? But where am I?" Lucky looked around in the shifting darkness.

"It's almost over," Alfie growled, turning away. "Can't you feel it?"

Lucky was silent, waiting for a shiver in his fur or a sense in his gut—but there was nothing.

Alfie's voice grew softer. "The Pack may still survive, as long as every dog does their duty when the Storm comes. Yours will be the most important of all."

Lucky couldn't help the whine that came out of his throat. "What duty?"

Alfie turned back to him. The thickset dog looked old and tired suddenly, his body beginning to fade into the swirling mist.

Lucky sprang forward. "Don't go, Alfie!" The ground groaned beneath his paws, and his ears were filled with the sound of cracking ice. Terror shot through Lucky's fur as the ground shattered beneath him, caving into a great hole. . . .

Instantly he was on his paws, blinking into the darkness. His heart raced in his chest and he gulped for air. Sweet still slept peacefully by his side. *It was just a dream.*

A thickset dog skulked outside the den. Lucky caught a flash of dark fur as he disappeared between the shrubs.

Alfie . . . ?

No, Alfie was dead. *This* must be the mysterious dog he had seen before, near the cliffs. Lucky rose silently, stepping around Sweet. He paused at the entrance to the den, wondering if he should wake her. *No. I'm a Beta now; I have to prove I can act on my own initiative.* He padded into the icy night, sniffing the air.

A bank of clouds blocked the light of the Moon-Dog. Dart, who was the Patrol Dog watching over the camp tonight, was nowhere in sight, no doubt out pacing the boundaries of their territory. Lucky put his trust in his nose, following the scent of the strange dog. It was maddeningly familiar, but the salt wind that drifted from the Endless Lake made it hard for him to place where he'd smelled it before. Lucky frowned, treading a path between low hedges. Could this be a Lone Dog? But why would *any* dog want to settle so close to a Pack?

His head snapped up. He realized with surprise that the smell had grown stronger—the dog up ahead must have stopped.

Lucky paused, sniffing carefully. He couldn't smell any other dogs. He decided to press ahead, scrambling beneath a dangling branch until the scent struck him all at once.

Fang!

Just then, the young Fierce Dog stepped out from behind a tree, wobbling badly. Lucky took in his appearance with a gasp. Storm's litter-brother had a wounded paw that still seemed to be bleeding from a deep bite. He stumbled, and Lucky sprang forward and gave him a gentle nudge to keep him upright.

"You'd help me, after everything?" Fang whimpered. His voice cracked as he spoke, and he looked exhausted. Slowly he settled down onto his hindquarters.

Lucky took a step back. "What happened?"

Fang lowered his head. "Mace attacked me when I tried to leave Blade's Pack. I got away, but not before he gave me a good bite. The Sun-Dog has run across the sky several times, but it hasn't quite healed." The young dog's head drooped. "I've been waiting by your camp, trying to work up the courage to ask for help healing the wound, but I lost my nerve." He sighed bitterly. "I waited for Dart to go patrol the boundaries, and then I sneaked into your camp. I didn't want you all thinking that I wanted to join your Pack. I know there's no chance of that. But I hoped that if some dog came to find out what was going on and followed me out of the camp, they might help."

Lucky narrowed his eyes. Fang had seemed intensely loyal to

the Fierce Dogs—and willing to kill his own litter-sister to prove it. What had changed? "Why did you leave Blade's Pack?"

Fang lowered himself onto his belly. Lucky had never seen the young dog looking so dejected. "In the Trial of Rage, Storm proved she was a better fighter than me, and that she had more self-control too. After that, Blade was furious that she had to honor the agreement to let Storm go. She said it was all my fault that we had been humiliated by 'inferior' dogs. She encouraged every dog in the Pack to torment me." His lip twitched into a snarl. "It would have been better if Storm had killed me." He fell quiet for a moment, then looked up at Lucky. "And it's not just me they're after. They're plotting against your Pack. I guess I wanted to warn you. You helped me a lot, in the beginning—you and Mickey. I didn't want Blade to track you down."

Lucky's fur bristled. "She's planning an ambush?"

A night bird hooted from a nearby tree and Fang jumped, his eyes jerking toward the sound. He scrambled shakily to his paws. "It isn't safe to talk here. I've made a temporary camp and it's hidden. Blade knows nothing about it. It isn't far. I'll take you there and explain, if . . . if you think you can help me?" Fang took a step forward and faltered, his face contorting with pain.

Lucky hurried to his side. "Here, lean on me."

They moved slowly around the outskirts of the valley, past the pond and the circle of trees. Lucky panted with effort as he helped Fang along. He could feel the weight of the Fierce Dog's muscles packed beneath his fur.

"It's not much farther," muttered Fang through gritted teeth. "Down along the cliffs."

By the time they reached the cliff face, Lucky's body blazed with heat, despite the icy wind. He helped Fang limp along the sharp rocks. It was barren along the wall of the cliff, open to the cold and rain. Surely no dog would sleep without shelter when it was this cold? Lucky looked at Fang, whose eyes were half-closed in pain. "Are you so afraid of the Fierce Dogs that you've made your camp *here*?"

A snarl behind him made him stumble in shock. "No . . . but Fang *is* so afraid of us that he'll lead his former protector into a trap."

CHAPTER FIVE

Lucky's heart lurched, and he spun around. His pulse raced as he took in the sight of Blade flanked by Mace and Dagger. Paws scuffled behind him, and Lucky looked back toward Fang. The rest of the Fierce Dog Pack stood behind the young Fierce Dog in formation, their muscles flexing beneath their silky coats. Panic coursed through Lucky's limbs. The only escape was over the cliff, where the Endless Lake hammered rocks as sharp as teeth. There was nowhere to run.

The Fierce Dogs had him surrounded!

"Take him," Blade snarled.

Mace and Dagger marched toward Lucky. He flinched, expecting to feel their fangs sink into his flesh. Instead the Fierce Dog deputies shoved him roughly along the edge of the cliff.

Lucky's heart sank. Ahead was a jumble of jagged black rocks.

Mace and Dagger shoved Lucky toward them as he cast about wildly for a way to escape. The rest of the Fierce Dogs closed in behind him. As Dagger butted him closer to the rocks, Lucky spotted a shadowy opening. A cave! It cut downhill, through the cliff. Lucky felt a rough shove against his flank, and he slid down the incline, kicking up pebbles. It was dark and dank in the cave, and it smelled sharply of the attack dogs.

This must be where they've made their new lair.

Lucky had no choice but to shuffle along the tunnel. Mace snapped at his flank, drawing him deeper into the lair. As Lucky's eyes adjusted to the darkness, he stared around desperately but could see no gaps or cracks of light along the stone walls.

"Hurry up, Street Mutt!" snarled Mace, slamming Lucky's flank with his forepaw and sending him smacking into the wall.

Lucky whined as pain shot through his shoulder, and he scrambled forward. The tunnel bent like a dog's leg, growing darker. Lucky could hardly see where he was going, but the smell of the Fierce Dogs was all around him. *The Pack must have come here when the longpaws returned to the town,* he realized. *They've probably been watching us for days.*

He cursed himself. How had he missed their odors on the icy air? "Move forward, you clumsy idiot!" snapped Mace.

Lucky quickened his stride. Here, a few chinks in the cave ceiling let in the faint light of the Moon-Dog, who had appeared between the clouds. Lucky squinted. There was something up ahead—it looked like a dark pool. As he drew closer, he could see it was a steep drop. He froze, his heart slamming against his ribs. In the weak light, he couldn't make out the bottom. *They're going to push me to my death!* he realized with cold horror. *The others will never find out what happened to me. Sweet will call for me, and I won't be there. . . .* He tried to conjure up an image of the Forest-Dog, to call him for help, but it was impossible to imagine trees down here in the musty air.

Lucky felt breath on the back of his neck, and his fur stood on end. Mace's muzzle was close to his ear. "I said, *forward!*"

There was a scuffle of paws, and Lucky turned to see Blade pressing alongside Mace, her eyes glinting with satisfaction. Her voice was silky. "This has been a long time coming, Street Mutt. Do you have any last words?"

"Don't do this." Lucky was ashamed of the whine in his voice. No: She wouldn't force him to be a coward. He swallowed down a mouthful of spit. He wouldn't beg for mercy. "I have *nothing* to say to you."

There was a note of disappointment in Blade's voice. "So long,

Mongrel!" She lurched at him, her teeth bared. Lucky sprang back instinctively, his paws scrambling for a moment above the dark drop. He fell with a bark, his legs flailing. His head hit the ground with a jolt of pain. Then he felt nothing.

The air smelled of ashes and bitter smoke. Lucky looked out over the broken longpaw city. Fires crackled on street corners, despite the driving rain that fell from the Sky-Dogs. Gray dust swirled in the air and caught in Lucky's throat. It shifted in dark palls, blocking out the light of the Sun-Dog. Somehow Lucky knew he would never feel the dazzling warmth of the Sun-Dog again—that the great Spirit Dog had retreated to the edges of their world.

Fierce Dogs marched side by side along the broken streets. Their sharp barks cut through the air and Lucky whined in fear, but they ignored him as they passed, as though he was invisible.

Lucky trembled under the rain, searching for shelter. He passed the Food House where he used to beg for scraps. But there were no scraps—the longpaws had long since gone. The city belonged to the Fierce Dogs now.

No dog should "own" the city, *thought Lucky.* Why doesn't the Earth-Dog growl again to chase them away, or teach them a lesson? *He tapped the ground with a forepaw, and his tail clung to his flank. He couldn't feel the Earth-Dog beneath him. The ground was cold, lifeless, and still. It was as if the Earth-Dog had been knocked out.*

Lucky heard an angry bark, and he spun around to see Mace and Dagger behind a group of dogs. The dogs' heads were stooped, and their tails hung low.

"Keep moving, Slaves!" snarled Mace, chomping and snapping at their legs.

Lucky's eyes rested on a golden-furred dog. She looked familiar, but her coat was patchy and thin and she struggled to walk. One of her hind legs was hideously misshapen, bent the wrong way. "Bella!" he cried. "Bella, what happened?"

His litter-sister did not turn around.

He noticed an old brown fight-dog and a small dog with wiry fur. Bruno and Daisy! Lucky gasped. The Slave Dogs were his old Pack, but they looked so injured, starved, and exhausted that he hardly recognized them. Mickey was leaning against Martha for support, and even the great black dog could hardly walk. Then Lucky noticed Sweet. . . .

Sickness twisted in his gut. The swift-dog's ribs jutted under loose flesh, and her legs were like bent twigs. There was a tear along her hip that was bleeding badly.

Blood was running down Dagger's chin.

Lucky reeled with fury. "Leave her alone!" he howled, but they didn't seem to hear him. He tried to run to Sweet, but his legs were fixed to the ground. He looked down to see red liquid sloshing over his paws.

Where was it coming from? His eyes shot up. The Fierce Dogs were gnashing and biting at the Wild Pack to keep them moving. They plodded past a giant heap of dark fur, as big as a loudcage—no, as big as the entire Wild Pack camp—that was half-buried beneath rubble. The stream of blood was flowing from the heap, winding along the broken street and lapping at Lucky's paws.

Blade bounded onto the heap of fur, climbing to the top and standing proudly as the fires burned around her. But what was she standing on? Could it really be . . .

Lucky blinked, shaking his head in disbelief.

Yes, it was—Blade had conquered the Earth-Dog!

Lucky tore his gaze away, only to find himself suddenly caged, staring at a wall of the Trap House. His muzzle was pressed up to the wire door of his cage as the other dogs slept around him. It was silent and still in the Trap House, but there was a faint quiver in the air. Something was coming.

Lucky pawed at the cage door, then shrank back, confused. Why do I keep returning here?

Alfie appeared in the passage between the cages and gazed up at Lucky. His voice was soft. "It's okay. You know what to do."

Lucky pawed the wire. "I don't! You have to tell me!"

His barks had woken the other dogs. The Trap House filled with whines and yaps as the ground started trembling beneath their paws.

"Alfie, won't you help me?" Lucky barked. "What do I have to do?" He threw himself at the wire, his face smacking the metal and his eyes clamped shut.

When he opened them, the Trap House was red. Liquid clung to Lucky's muzzle and ran down his whiskers. The taste was foul, like ash and spoiled meat. He knew what it was.

It was the Earth-Dog's blood.

Lucky opened his eyes and blinked into the darkness. *I'm alive!* Salty water dripped onto his forehead and rolled down his nose. He raised his pounding head and looked to the ceiling. He was in a deep bowl, a cave within a cave in the Fierce Dogs' lair, somewhere inside the cliff. It reminded him of the hollow pathway that the rescue party had discovered in the cliff nearest to the Wild Pack's territory, the one they'd climbed through to escape the Endless Lake. His head throbbed where he'd hit it from the fall, but otherwise he seemed okay. He stretched his legs gingerly—nothing seemed broken.

He stood up and looked around. There was an opening in the ceiling of the cave, and Lucky could see the Moon-Dog and the first creeping light of the Sun-Dog.

A wave of relief ran through him. The Sun-Dog was still safe—the Fierce Dogs hadn't banished him yet. He caught himself and frowned. *That was just a bad dream. For all their might, the Fierce Dogs could never attack the Spirit Dogs. Their teeth aren't that big.*

The air was salty. There was probably a stream nearby, running into the Endless Lake. That would explain the water dripping from the ceiling. Lucky padded toward the edge of the cave bowl and hopped onto his hind legs, searching for a way out. The walls were too steep to climb. He tried to hook his paws on the ragged rock face, but he couldn't get a clawhold.

Behind him, he heard an amused growl. Lucky turned to see Blade standing in the tunnel over the rock bowl. She glared down at Lucky.

"I hope you had sweet dreams," she rasped. There was a kind of frenzied victory in the Fierce Dog Alpha's eyes.

Lucky could barely stand to look at her. "If you're so determined to destroy the Wild Pack, why didn't you kill me when you caught me?" he spat. "You must be going soft!"

Blade stepped to the edge of the bowl and lowered her head menacingly. "Don't underestimate me, Street Mutt. I'm every bit as ruthless as I need to be, and I intend to prove it." She snorted through her nose. "Do you really think I'd go to so much trouble just to kill *you*? It seems that being made a Beta has gone to your head."

Lucky's face must have given away his surprise. How did she know?

"Oh, I know everything you've been up to," she hissed. "Fang saw your touching little ceremony with the skinny swift-dog. Don't get me wrong. In some ways, she impresses me. She's tough, and she runs an efficient Pack, for a group of mutts. Unfortunately she's also dumb, like all Wild Dogs. She lacks *discipline*."

A low growl rose in Lucky's throat. Fear still consumed him, but another sensation tingled through his whiskers—*anger.* "Leave her out of this!"

Blade shook her head slowly and ran a self-satisfied tongue over her chops. She dropped onto her belly and lowered her muzzle so it hung over the edge of the rock bowl. "It's too late for that. What do you imagine happened the minute your Pack-rats realized you were missing? It won't be hard for them to track you here, not with Fang's blood dripping a trail. Loyalty without intelligence—that's the problem with you Wild Dogs. She'll walk right into my trap."

"Leave Sweet alone, she's no danger to you!" Lucky barked, his head still pounding.

Blade threw back her head. "You stupid idiot! Do you think I care about your skinny Alpha? It's the Fierce pup I'm after. I will rip out her throat and stop her from doing more harm." Her voice was brittle. "I will *eliminate* the threat."

A chill ran down Lucky's spine. "What do you mean, 'the threat'? Storm doesn't want to take over your Pack. She's no threat to you as long as you leave her alone!"

"You're wrong," growled Blade. "That young dog will destroy us—Fierce Dogs, Wild Dogs, Leashed Dogs, *all of us*. I have seen it in my dreams."

Lucky's breath caught in his throat and he froze, stunned. Hadn't he also guessed that Storm had a role to play in their downfall? He thought of telling Blade about his own dreams. Had she also seen the Storm of Dogs, the terrible battle in the swirling snow? He pulled himself together with a violent shake of the fur. Blade was just afraid of losing a fight with Storm. It probably had nothing to do with the Storm of Dogs, nothing to do with his visions. . . .

Blade's eyes were wild. "I have seen it—the end of this world. Just as when the Big Growl came and lakes of blood poured from the Earth-Dog's wounds; I foresaw that too! Now she is in pain and furious. Only more blood will avenge her wounds!" She bared her teeth, growling low in her throat. "A young Fierce Dog will bring about the final battle, the fight that will tear the sky in two and fill the world with snow and blood. There is only one way to stop it, and the Spirit Dogs have shown me what to do. I must destroy the Fierce Dog pups born after the Growl. The Earth-Dog demands a sacrifice, and if she doesn't get it, she will growl again and kill us all!"

Lucky stumbled, sick to his stomach. Dizzily, he remembered the dead pup he and Mickey had found in the Dog-Garden. He hadn't been from Storm and Fang's litter. "You killed your own pup," he gasped.

Blade flinched, as though struck. Then her face grew grim. "I did what I had to."

"And Wiggle . . ." Lucky's heart ached when he thought of that small, vulnerable puppy—the weakest and gentlest of the Fierce Dog litter the Pack had rescued.

Blade was unrepentant. "I would kill him again. I was careless when my Pack left the Dog-Garden. I killed the Mother-Dog and assumed that the pups would weaken and die without her. *You* were the one who stole them away and ruined my plans, but I will make it right. The Spirit Dogs have spoken, and I will not shirk my duty again." She rose to her paws. "It is up to me to prevent another Big Growl. First I will put down Storm—and then I will kill her worthless brother. I promise, though, I'll make his death quick—he did well to help put this trap in place."

She turned and barked down the tunnel. "Arrow!"

Lucky heard the scrambling of paws. A moment later he saw the outline of a young Fierce Dog, not much older than Storm and Fang. He wore no collar, unlike the rest of his Pack. But his ears were pointed like a sharpclaw's, without the jagged edges of Fang's torn flesh. A longpaw must have cut them with brutal precision. That meant the young dog was born before the Big Growl. He stood at attention obediently, waiting for Blade to give her orders. *I wonder if he realizes how close he came to being killed by her?* Lucky wondered. *If he'd been born after that awful day.*

"Are you ready?" asked Blade.

"Yes, Alpha!" barked Arrow.

The two Fierce Dogs disappeared down the tunnel.

Lucky's head was still spinning. He had to get out, to warn his Packmates that this was a trap—but how? He cocked his head, thinking. The far wall seemed to be a little more rugged, and dipped at a slight incline. If he could just get enough speed . . . He ran at the wall with all his might, jumping as he reached it and throwing his forepaws against it, but the rock was too hard and smooth for a decent grip. He slipped back down and hit the ground with a thud.

Struggling to keep calm and to control his frustration, Lucky took a deep breath and started circling the wall. Where water trailed over the stones, there were small clumps of moss. *Maybe I can climb up on those.*

He tested the moss with his paws. Some of it fell away under pressure, but the rest seemed firmly connected to the stone. *If I can climb it quickly, before it collapses . . .*

Lucky backed up as far as he could, then ran at the wall. He sank his claws into the moss, feeling the soft earthy greenery crumble away beneath his paws. It held just long enough to let him scurry up the stone.

I'm doing it! I'm almost out!

He threw his forepaws over the top of the cave bowl with a rush of euphoria, preparing to pull himself up.

The gleam of fangs flashed overhead, and pain shot through Lucky's forepaw.

CHAPTER SIX

Lucky howled, squinting up against the darkness. He could make out the ragged, wolfish outline of a head at the top of the rock bowl. *Alpha! Our old Alpha!* The dog-wolf crunched down on Lucky's flesh with a growl of triumph.

Fire seared through Lucky's paw and he lost his footing, tumbling back down the rock face and smacking his side against the damp floor of the cave. Salt water splashed the wound, and Lucky swallowed an agonized yelp. He clenched his teeth. *I won't give the half wolf the satisfaction!*

The former leader of the Wild Pack prowled the edge of the stone dip. Against the opening to the sky, his long face was in shadow, but Lucky could see a wicked glint in those cold yellow eyes.

"You'll never learn," the wolf-dog snarled. "Always wanting to play the hero. How dumb *are* you? To fall for such an obvious trick. How could you trust Fang, after everything that's happened? You can't trust *every* dog."

"I know *that's* true," Lucky snarled back, doing his best to stand upright despite the throbbing in his paw. "I knew you were rotten at heart from the moment I saw you. You killed Alfie."

The dog-wolf stopped pacing. *"Alfie?"* He seemed genuinely confused.

Lucky bristled with rage. *He doesn't even remember his name! That's how little Alfie meant to him.*

The dog-wolf cocked his head in thought. "Oh . . . that tubby little Leashed Dog? He was on my territory without permission. He and his motley Pack were a threat to the Wild Dogs. It had to be that way."

Lucky howled. "You killed a good dog, and you don't even have the decency to feel remorse. You're evil! You enjoy tricking other dogs and getting the better of them, just like you love seeing me in this trap."

The half wolf leaned over the rim of the rock bowl, baring his fangs. "You don't know anything," he snarled. "It has never been about *you*."

"Oh really?" Lucky scoffed. "What is it about, then? What is it that makes you turn on your own Pack and join the Fierce Dogs?"

The dog-wolf glanced warily along the tunnel. He lowered his voice. "It's about survival. I will do whatever it takes to stay alive. If more dogs thought like me, we'd all be better off."

Lucky sighed. "But the Wild Pack was okay. The Leashed Dogs had joined, everyone was getting along. When you fell in the Endless Lake, we all thought you were dead. The Pack *grieved* for you." *Well, most of them did.* Lucky had to admit that he hadn't felt that sorry when the half wolf disappeared. "Then you go and join the Fierce Dogs! You hate them! It doesn't make any sense."

The half wolf's voice was low. "It's true that I *used* to hate the Fierce Dogs for their cruelty. I didn't like how they were trained to be the teeth and violence of the longpaws. That's how I'd known them before the Big Growl—as Longpaw Fangs." He threw a furtive look over his shoulder. "They're different now. They don't answer to anyone. When my Pack grew to include Leashed Dogs, I saw how easily things fell apart between them. The Fierce Dogs stick together. I respect Blade. I admire her clear thinking and authority and the discipline of her Pack."

Lucky shook his head in frustration. "So you're prepared to cower and beg to them? To run errands and eat last?"

"I don't intend to stay Omega forever." The former Alpha ran his tongue over his teeth. Lucky could see the silvery sheen of the wolf-dog's fur. The Sun-Dog was rising. "Talent plays a part in success, even in this Pack. Who do you think came up with the plan to get you down here?"

Lucky could hardly control his fury, but he raised his muzzle and kept his voice steady. "Omega. That's your name these days, isn't it?"

The half wolf's lip twitched with anger. "That's not my name. Neither is Alpha. You will never know my *real* name." He opened his mouth to say more, but his ears pricked up and he tensed as Arrow appeared along the far tunnel, a jagged piece of driftwood in his jaws. The wolf-dog shrank away like a scolded pup, disappearing along the tunnel. Lucky watched as Arrow placed the wood on the edge of the rocks where the Fierce Dogs' Omega had stood, making it impossible to climb out.

Arrow went about his business as though Lucky wasn't there. He finished dragging the wood into position and marched back along the tunnel, leaving Lucky alone.

The wind was rising over the Endless Lake. Lucky could hear the crash and churn of water not far away and smell the sharp salt air. He shivered with cold, unable to find any shelter in the damp cave.

He gave a little whine and tried shaking his fur for warmth, as Moon had taught him to do. It didn't seem to help anymore. He paced about the cave, his paws splashing through icy water. Gazing into the sky, he saw that the Moon-Dog had vanished, but the Sun-Dog was only a faint tail of light below dark-gray clouds. What had happened to the Spirit Dogs? Lucky had once felt confident in their protection, but ever since the Earth-Dog had growled, he had grown less and less sure.

How do my dreams about the Storm of Dogs fit into it all? He remembered with a start what Blade had said. *She has seen the same things—she knows that Storm will be involved somehow.* Now he was even more worried that what they had seen was not just dreams, but something else. *They must be messages from the Spirit Dogs.* Yet Storm herself seemed unaware of the danger. *If the dreams are omens from the Spirit Dogs, why are they warning me? And Blade? Why doesn't Storm sense this terrible future, if she is to play such an important role?*

And what will my role be when the time comes?

The Sun-Dog was hovering straight above the hole in the roof of the cave. Lucky watched him sorrowfully, wishing the great Spirit Dog would send down some heat. Icy water from the Endless Lake streamed down from the roof, swishing about his paws. It rose in deep puddles before gradually seeping away. Lucky's paws were now constantly under the water, and at its worst it crept up his flank.

What if it stops draining away? I'll drown in this miserable pit.

His belly growled with hunger, and his throat was cracked and dry with thirst. He knew better than to drink the water that surrounded him. *Salt water just makes things worse.* His head felt faint and his legs quivered, both from weakness and cold.

He pressed his side against the rock wall, trying to stay upright and keep as much of his fur dry as possible. The clouds had lifted, and a cruel wind cut down from the cliff. Against the sting of the air, the salt water bit like teeth. He raised his injured paw, licking it regularly. Sadness washed over him. With great effort and longing, he pictured trees in the rich, gentle haze of summer. He remembered his favorite Spirit Dog, who had guided him to safety so many times.

Wise Forest-Dog, do not leave me alone to despair in the terrible cold. I will be the bravest dog in this world, the humblest and most loyal, if you help me escape—if I could see your forests once more.

He imagined the sweet dew that hung from leaves and pictured it dripping down into his open mouth. His head sank against the rock, and his mind blurred. The salt water that splashed his muzzle was nothing like dew. It stung his whiskers, but he no longer had the energy to flinch from each drop. Ice Wind's chill fangs cut into his flesh and his body jerked in violent shivers, his breath coming in fast snorts.

"Lucky!"

Through the fog in his head, Lucky looked up. A slim, elegant dog stood high above him. *Sweet?* Was it a dream?

Bella appeared at her side, peering over the pile of driftwood that Arrow had left behind. It wasn't a dream—they were here to save him! Down here, among the rocks, where nothing grew, the Forest-Dog had heard him!

There was a shuffle of paws overhead, and a broad, dark face joined Bella and Sweet.

Storm—she came with them. . . .

Lucky's joy evaporated, and icy dread ran through his limbs. If only this *was* a dream. Because if it was real—if Sweet and the others had come to rescue him—it meant Blade's evil plan had worked.

CHAPTER SEVEN

Lucky heard scrabbling overhead as Sweet, Bella, and Storm worked to pull away the driftwood.

They're really here.

"No," rasped Lucky. His voice cracked and he swallowed hard, trying to force out the words, to warn his friends that they'd walked into Blade's trap.

"It's okay," Bella soothed. "Try not to speak." She reached down a paw and patted the dip in the wall. "Jump onto your hind legs if you can."

Lucky's head was spinning and his vision was blurry. He tried to focus on his litter-sister. With a deep breath, he threw his forepaws onto the rock wall. Storm appeared overhead, her head cocked anxiously. Lucky's hind legs were trembling badly, and he could hardly keep upright. He shut his eyes and tried to ignore the pain as Storm closed her strong jaws around his neck and tugged him up the wall. He sensed Sweet and Bella pressing closer, and soon they had dragged him over the rock lip and into the tunnel.

Lucky collapsed in a heap in front of them, gasping for breath. There was a pool of water in front of his nose, and he sniffed it carefully. Rain! He lapped it up, feeling the clean, icy water slip down his throat. He gave silent thanks to the Forest-Dog. *He may be far away, but he has not deserted me.*

Sweet licked Lucky's face. "You're okay now. We're here, and we're going to take you home."

His voice came out a pathetic whine. "You don't understand. Blade *wanted* you to find me. It's a trap."

Storm shook her head firmly. "We scouted out the route before we came into this. There's no dog here."

Lucky sat up, then climbed to his feet, feeling refreshed by the rainwater. He sniffed the air furtively, but there was no hint of the Fierce Dogs. He allowed a trickle of hope to run through him. *Maybe Storm's right. Could Blade have let down her guard?*

A snarl echoed along the passageway. "I knew it. You dogs are too loyal and too foolish to keep away."

Lucky and the others turned to see the sharp outline of Blade's pointed ears. She stood farther down the corridor, her Pack lined up in orderly rows behind her. Their coats shimmered wetly. *They must have rolled in water from the Endless Lake,* Lucky realized. *That's why we couldn't smell them.*

Sweet threw a look at the jagged rock bowl, then back toward the Fierce Dogs. "We have to run straight at them," she murmured. "There's a place to turn along the passage in front of them—a sort of side tunnel. If we surprise the Fierce Dogs by running at them, we can turn into it before they know what's happening. We can give ourselves a head start."

Bella gave a quick nod. "We'll have to be fast to reach it before they do."

Lucky stiffened, preparing to follow. He still felt giddy, and his legs trembled with cold and fatigue. *I'm not sure I can run.*

There was no time to share his worries. Sweet burst forward, pounding toward the Fierce Dogs. Blade's jaw dropped in surprise as the swift-dog flew toward her along the tunnel. Bella and Storm scampered after their Alpha, and Lucky followed, struggling to command his shaking legs. It was impossible for any of them to keep up with Sweet, but he was falling behind badly.

"Prepare to die, bully dogs!" Sweet bluffed.

Looking up ahead, he could see confusion cross Blade's face. *She doesn't know what Sweet's planning to do—she hasn't guessed yet. She can't* believe a Wild Dog would dare attack her in front of her Pack. Blade's confusion gave the swift-dog the advantage. Sweet looked as if she was about to throw herself at Blade, but instead she changed direction and sprang down the side tunnel, away from the Fierce Dogs.

Blade's eyes widened with rage. "After them!" she barked.

The Fierce Dogs charged. They were powering down the passageway straight at Bella, Storm, and Lucky.

"Do what you like to the Mongrel Rats!" cried Blade. "But don't let the pup go! *I want the pup!*"

Bella had picked up pace. She turned the corner and disappeared down the side tunnel, reaching it before the Fierce Dogs. Storm was not far behind Bella, and Lucky was fighting to stay with her, tripping on his exhausted legs. *We have to follow Sweet and Bella into the side tunnel before Blade reaches it!* He gritted his teeth and ran through the pain. He found he was gaining on Storm. *She's slowing down,* he realized with surprise. *Why would she . . . ?*

A tremor of fear ran through him as he realized Storm *wanted* the Fierce Dogs to catch up with her. *She doesn't want to run—she wants to fight!*

Somehow this thought gave Lucky the surge he needed to catch up with Storm. "Come with me!" he barked. "We need to stay with Sweet. We haven't gone this far to fail now!" He caught her eye and saw rage there.

"I have a score to settle with Blade!" she snarled.

"Now is not the time for that! There's too many of them! Do you want Sweet and Bella to get hurt? Do you want to die yourself?" With a wince he forced himself to run faster, doing his best to ignore the pain in his forepaw. To his relief, Storm drew up alongside him, picking up speed. They scrambled into the side tunnel just ahead of the furious Fierce Dogs.

We're going to make it! thought Lucky with a burst of elation.

But something was wrong. Sweet and Bella had stopped up ahead. Lucky and Storm slammed to a halt, panting heavily.

Lucky squinted through the gloom. His heart thumped, and his tail was stiff behind him. He could see the thick shapes of three Fierce Dogs. Their heavy collars glinted at their necks—all except the middle dog, who wasn't wearing one. He was smaller than the others, barely more than a puppy, but his thickly muscled body made him look much older. Lucky recognized the roughly cut ears—torn by the teeth of another dog. *Fang* . . .

He heard the scuffle of paws and turned to see Blade and the rest of her Pack. It was no use—there was nowhere left to run.

Storm's hackles rose and she dropped her head, a growl in her throat. Ignoring her littermate, she squared up to Blade. "This is how you act, with trickery and deceit!" she barked. "You're not even brave enough for a fair fight." She took a step toward the Fierce Dog Alpha, but Sweet and Bella leaped in front of her, blocking her way.

"Stay calm," urged Sweet in a low voice.

Storm's voice quivered with rage. "I should have known. The leader of the Fierce Dogs is nothing but a *pathetic coward!*"

Blade became very still, her eyes wide with outrage. "You run with the Mongrel Rats!" she spat. "How dare *you* accuse *me* of dishonor?"

Lucky licked Storm's ear, trying to coax her to keep calm. "Blade wants you to fight," he reminded her. Then he remembered what the Fierce Dog Alpha had told him.

A young Fierce Dog will bring about the final battle, the one that will tear the sky in two and fill the world with snow and blood.

Fear crept along Lucky's spine. Blade didn't want Storm to fight—she wanted her to *die.*

The leader of the Fierce Dogs lifted her muzzle. "Fang, get over here," she snapped. "By my side, you'll have the best view of your litter-sister's death."

The young Fierce Dog gave a quick nod. He started limping toward Blade, pressing between Sweet and Bella. He passed his litter-sister, keeping his gaze straight ahead.

Lucky couldn't help feeling sorry for Fang, despite everything. He remembered the spirited, bright-eyed pup that he and Mickey had rescued from the Dog-Garden. Fang was nothing like that anymore—his skin hung loosely in rolls of fur, and the deep bite marks were raw. Every movement seemed to cause the young dog pain. *They've destroyed him,* thought Lucky, sorrow running through him to the tip of his tail. *If only he'd stayed with us.*

Fang limped up to Blade and sat awkwardly by her side. The Alpha's eyes glinted in the half-light as she ran a tongue over her jagged teeth.

Lucky sighed. *He wanted to be with his own kind. Even after he saw Blade kill Wiggle.* Lucky's muscles tensed. Why *had* Blade kept Fang alive? *He was born after the Big Growl, just like his littermates.*

Lucky frowned, his skin crawling as he remembered what Blade had said before—about how she would make Fang's death quick. She had not yet "put down" Storm, but Blade had never been one to ignore an opportunity to cause destruction whenever it suited her.

"Fang!" Lucky barked urgently. "Run! Get out of here!"

Before the young Fierce Dog could react, Blade swung around without warning and sank her teeth into Fang's throat, ripping the fur away savagely. Fang's blood spurted from his throat in wide arcs, splashing against the walls of the tunnel. A horrible gurgling sound came from the pulsing red tear. The young dog jerked and thrashed, collapsing onto his side. His back legs pumped and his forepaws scraped the tunnel wall, red with his own blood.

Storm gave a horrified yelp, but for a moment, no other dog made a sound.

Lucky was frozen to the spot, watching with horror as Fang started trembling violently, the way Terror used to when he claimed he had visions from the Spirit Dogs. But the young Fierce Dog wasn't having visions.

Fang was dying.

Blade loomed over him triumphantly.

Every dog was stunned by what they were seeing. The Fierce Dogs stood silently as the dogs from the Wild Pack cringed with fear. But Blade was victorious. She shoved Fang toward the wall with her strong paw and started licking the blood off her coat. Fang shook violently, his eyes rolling back so they looked smooth and white as the Moon-Dog. With a last gurgle, his head lolled and his body fell still.

"You killed him," Lucky gasped. "He was loyal to you—and you *killed him*."

Blade slammed down her paw. "This has *nothing* to do with loyalty. I am saving every dog—you should be grateful!" She cast a sharp look at her own Pack. "The Spirit Dogs have spoken. The pups born after the Growl came must be put down. Now, all but one of them has." Blade's eyes were wild. She licked the last of Fang's blood off her dark whiskers. The Fierce Dog Alpha stared at Storm. "It is time to put an end to this. It is time for the last of the pups to die."

Lucky moved to block Blade's path. He glanced back warily at Storm.

The shock was dissolving from the young Fierce Dog's face, and instead her muzzle twisted with anger as she lifted her gaze from the bloodied body of her litter-brother. Butting Lucky out of the way with her powerful muscles, she charged at Blade.

Blade dropped her head, preparing to run at Storm. Then she looked up quite unexpectedly. "Something's happening!" she breathed.

Storm had stopped in her tracks, her head whipping left and right.

Lucky could feel it too. The air was shivering, and the urge to run was almost unbearable. His fur tingled and he looked to Sweet. The swift-dog's jaw fell open and her eyes grew round. "It's like in the Trap House, just before the walls started shaking."

Mace shrank against the wall, and Dagger whined like a pup. "It's like before! When the longpaws left!"

"What is it?" barked Storm. She stared down at her paws. "It feels like Earth-Dog is shaking her fur! Is she angry? Is she sick?" She sprang back, turning to Lucky. "Why does every dog seem to know what's going on except me?"

"Because it's happened before," murmured Lucky. Of course Storm couldn't know—she'd been born after the Big Growl. She had heard about it, but she couldn't have guessed how it felt. There was no time to explain. He whispered urgently to Sweet and Bella, "We need to get out while the Fierce Dogs are distracted." Sweet burst forward first, her light paws pounding a path over the trembling ground. Bella ran after her, zigzagging past the Fierce Dogs, who were too stunned to stop her. Lucky gave Storm a shove. "Run!" He didn't wait for her reply as he charged along the tunnel and was relieved to hear her pounding pawsteps behind him.

The ground still quivered beneath their paws. "Earth-Dog has spoken!" barked Blade. "This is a warning—she will send the Big Growl to destroy us all if the pup escapes!"

Lucky threw a look over his shoulder. Mace was sniffing the ground, his thin tail clinging to his leg. Dagger started along the tunnel after the Wild Dogs but paused, one paw suspended in front of him. "The air is trembling!" he whined.

"I don't care what the air is doing! Get the pup!" howled Blade, but her Pack recoiled in fear.

They're not coming after us! thought Lucky with a surge of relief. It gave him the energy to push on. Turning back to Storm and gritting his teeth against the pain in his paw, he hurried to bound alongside her. Together, they slipped around a dark corner to see Sweet and Bella escaping through a gap in the rocks, out into the open.

Lucky and Storm burst outside, gulping the clean, cold air. Their paws skidded on the hard earth, but the ground seemed more stable now. *Maybe the Earth-Dog won't growl again after all,* thought Lucky with a quiver of hope. He ran for his life, fighting to keep up with Sweet, Bella, and Storm.

He followed the other dogs over low hedges and around sharp boulders, cutting a path along the cliff and back over the valley toward the camp. Twigs lashed at his legs, and burs clung to his tail.

Sweet had come to a halt up ahead and was waiting for Storm and Lucky to catch up. Her eyes narrowed. "I don't think we've been followed."

"They will march straight to our camp to hunt down Storm," Bella muttered. "Blade seemed determined. And after what she did to Fang . . ."

Lucky dipped his head, still queasy at the thought of what they'd seen.

"I'm not scared of her," snarled Storm.

"You should be," Bella snapped.

Sweet started for the camp. "Come on. We need to have the Pack around us—we're still isolated up here." Her eyes fell on Lucky. "You look terrible. Hang in there, we're almost safe."

The Sun-Dog was bounding beyond the horizon as Lucky limped into camp, propped up by Bella and Storm. Sweet had run ahead and now greeted them with Sunshine, Mickey, and Daisy, who gathered around Lucky, offering their help.

"He needs to rest!" barked Mickey, his black-and-white head cocked with concern.

"What he needs is food!" yapped Sunshine.

Daisy licked Lucky's nose. "He's so *cold!*"

Sweet barked impatiently. "Bruno! Snap! Go and get him something to eat."

The hunt-dogs dipped their heads and bounded toward the trees as Lucky limped to his den. His body was trembling again, as it had in the cave. Deep, violent chills ran through him, and he struggled to stay upright. As he crept into the den, Bella, Sweet, and Storm squeezed themselves around him. He felt the warmth that rose from their fur, but his teeth still chattered and his body shuddered.

"You'll be okay soon," Sweet soothed, reaching over to lick his nose.

Lucky wasn't so sure. *I was cold for so long, my blood feels like it has turned to ice. Will I ever get warm again?*

CHAPTER EIGHT

Lucky's eyelids were heavy as he shook away the pelt of sleep and blinked into the darkness. His foreleg throbbed where the dog-wolf had bitten him, but at least he was warm now. Sweet, Bella, and Storm were still curled around him, sleeping deeply. *It's thanks to them that I escaped,* thought Lucky. *We're safe at the camp now. I should feel relieved.*

Instead a familiar sense of foreboding crept along his whiskers. There was a hint of something metallic in the air. The Earth-Dog was silent, but Lucky's neck fur still bristled; something was shifting beneath his paws.

A delicious smell tickled his nose, distracting him. All at once he realized how hungry he was. His belly growled, and he smacked his lips as Sunshine padded to the den's entrance. She held a breast piece torn from one of the plump geese. She trotted toward him and laid the meat at Lucky's paws.

Sweet opened one eye. "That's all yours, Beta," she murmured. "You need it. The rest of us will eat later." She closed her eye and let her head loll.

Lucky stared hungrily at the piece of bird.

"Bruno caught it specially for you," Sunshine explained. "We were all so worried—we knew you wouldn't have just left us, and when you didn't come back, we thought something terrible had happened."

Lucky cocked his head gratefully. He ran his tongue over his lips and tried to speak, but his voice cracked. He felt too weak and thirsty to eat.

Sunshine watched for a moment, her nose twitching with concern. She spun around and ducked out of the den. He could hear her scampering about outside, then a rustling and dragging sound. The dirty white dog reappeared, backing into the den with a piece of bark in her jaws. Lucky saw that it was curved like a bowl, water glistening inside it. As Sunshine set the bark in front of him, he fell upon the water and lapped it up thirstily.

"Thank you, Omega," he whispered. "I needed that."

She wagged her knotted white tail. "And now you need to eat something! You'll feel so much better for it." She tore off a mouthful of the prey-creature and fed it to Lucky. He chewed the tender morsel, feeling the juice run down his throat. Sunshine was right—he felt better already. The little dog continued to offer Lucky small chunks of meat, licking his nose as he gobbled them down. Then Lucky tensed, remembering Fang's brutal death. "Has there been any sign of the Fierce Dogs?"

"You're safe now," Sunshine murmured. "You're surrounded by the Pack, and we have Patrol Dogs everywhere. No one can get through. So you should just relax and get better."

Lucky let his eyes close. He hadn't felt cared for like this since he was a pup.

Yap sighed as his Mother-Dog licked his nose. He nuzzled against her coat, his belly round with milk and the soft meat that the longpaws put out for the Pup-Pack. The longpaw den was cozy. Light glanced through the clear-stone, warm against Yap's fur. He yawned contentedly and opened his eyes.

"Mother, will you tell me a story?"

Yap snuggled closer as his Mother-Dog rested a comforting paw across his back. "Very well. I will tell you about Lightning, the swiftest of the dog warriors."

Yap's tail gave a cheerful wag. This was one of his favorite stories!

His Mother-Dog cleared her throat. "The Sky-Dogs watched over Lightning and protected him. But Earth-Dog was jealous. She thought Lightning had lived too long and that it was time for him to die so that she could take his life force."

A chill crept over Yap. The beam of sunlight had disappeared. Clouds drifted outside the clear-stone, darkening the sky. His Mother-Dog's voice grew deeper, and her body stiffened.

"One night, Lightning began to tease the Earth-Dog. He was always a little wicked and crafty, clawing the ground quickly before racing back to the sky, where he was safe."

Yap craned his neck to look at his Mother-Dog in surprise. He knew that Lightning and the Sky-Dogs could be mischievous, but it was always in the spirit of fun. He'd never imagined that Lightning was actually mean to Earth-Dog.

The Mother-Dog's paw across Yap's shoulder felt heavier. "Earth-Dog had anticipated Lightning's tricks this time. She lay quietly, waiting, until the touch of Lightning's claws became so regular that she could predict where he was about to land next." Her voice became louder. "Earth-Dog waited and waited, licking her chops. When Lightning sprang down toward her, what do you think happened?"

Yap watched his Mother-Dog, wide-eyed.

She continued, her voice growing shrill. "With a terrible growl, Earth-Dog opened her mouth wide and swallowed Lightning whole!"

Yap gasped in shock. He'd heard this story before—and this wasn't how it was supposed to end! He buried his head in his Mother-Dog's coat. Her muscles flexed beneath the fur, and Yap pulled back, looking up at her for reassurance.

He whined in horror—it wasn't his Mother-Dog staring down at him.

It was Blade!

The Fierce Dog flashed her teeth and lowered her head to his so that their whiskers were almost touching. Her breath smelled metallic, like blood.

Yap cowered from her, but Blade pinned him to the ground, her paw bearing down on his back.

"What have you done with Mother?" Yap whined. "Where is my Pup-Pack?"

Blade's eyes sparkled gleefully. "Wicked dogs must be punished," she snarled. "The Earth-Dog swallowed Lightning whole! And the ground was soaked with blood."

Her paw against his back was so heavy he could hardly breathe.

Lucky's eyes snapped open to see the Sun-Dog beaming down on the den. He sprang to his paws, his heart racing. There was no sign of Blade beneath the bright-blue sky.

With a sigh of relief, he shook off the memories of his bad dream and looked around. Sweet, Storm, and Bella were no longer in the den. Lucky yawned and stretched out his legs. He wouldn't think about the nightmare, he told himself. His belly still felt pleasantly full, and his body was stronger after a good sleep. Even his paw hardly hurt anymore.

Lucky padded down to the pond between the trees. There he drank deeply. Outside the comfort of the den, the wind pierced Lucky's coat and he shivered. The trees were bare, and even the long grass by the pond bowed under frost. Lucky sniffed the ground.

The frost disguised scents, but there was a hint of something unusual down there. He sniffed again. A whiff of sourness came from the soil. The air hummed with a faint vibration. The fur rose along Lucky's back as he experienced a familiar sense of dread.

This is how it felt before the world fell apart. Earth-Dog was still unsettled—still dangerous. What would it take to appease her? Lucky thought with a shudder of Blade's dark prophecy. *She's wrong,* he told himself firmly. *This has nothing to do with Storm.* But his anxiety lingered.

I have to warn the others! We need to find somewhere safe.

He could hear barking toward the edge of the cliff, and he hurried to join the others. Sweet was gathered with the rest of the Pack. There was no need to warn them—they had guessed what was happening.

"We can all feel it," yapped Snap. "Shouldn't we get out of here?"

Dart, the little brown chase-dog, spun a quick, anxious circle.

"Last time the Growl tore down trees, and the ground . . . the ground just fell apart!"

Daisy's ears pricked up. "My longpaws' house shook and shook. And when I barked for them, they weren't there!"

"The clear-stone shattered!" barked Bruno, his brown ears flicking back. "It just shattered!"

Whine huddled low to the ground, his small body shaking.

The Pack started panicking, and Sweet barked loudly to silence them. "Dogs, stay calm. We all remember the Big Growl. There's nothing to be gained in dragging out bad memories."

Lucky came to her side. "We have to leave, to get as far away as possible."

"But where would we go?" Sweet gazed beyond the valley to the cliffs. "We could never outrun the Growl. At least it's fairly open here, and the trees are mostly by the pond. Don't you remember the longpaw city, or the town down by the Endless Lake? When the Earth-Dog shakes, tall and heavy things become *dangerous*. Isn't it better to be out in the open when the Growl arrives?"

Moon rose to her paws. "Alpha is right. Don't you all remember how the ground shook and the trees started falling in the forest? Most of us survived because our camp was in a clearing. We're better off staying in a more open space like this rather than trying to find a better place that we don't even know exists."

Dart whined and hid her head between her paws while Daisy hopped in circles.

Lucky thought about this. Sweet and Moon had a point. Where would they go? How could they escape the ground they walked on?

Sweet turned to him. "What do you think, Beta?"

He dipped his head. "I agree. We're better off staying where we are. We should probably keep away from the edge of the cliffs, though. In the Big Growl, some of the longpaw houses collapsed—it would be dangerous if the same thing happened to the cliffs and we were standing nearby." He thought of the longpaw town down by the Endless Lake. The streets had been covered in sand and river grass. Had the lake broken its bank during the Growl, spraying its water over everything? Lucky shuddered. "And we should keep our distance from the lake."

A calm fell over the Pack. *They are reassured by the agreement between their Alpha and Beta,* he realized.

Daisy stepped forward nervously, her tail pointed down to the ground. "What about the longpaws you saw in town?" she asked. "They're too close to the Endless Lake—the Growl will get them!"

Sweet's ears flicked back. "That isn't our problem. Sorry if it seems uncaring, but it isn't like they went out of their way to help *us*."

Original members of the Wild Pack were quick to agree.

"The longpaws think they're so clever," muttered Moon, her blue eyes cool as the sky. "Well, let them work it out for themselves."

Former Leashed Dogs looked less sure, exchanging worried glances. Mickey stepped forward. "Some of us lived with longpaws. They looked after us, they fed us, they even loved us." He paused, looking into the distance. Lucky wondered if the Farm Dog was picturing the young longpaw he had once thought of as his closest friend. Mickey appealed to Sweet. "Don't misunderstand me, I'm a Wild Dog now, we all are. I don't want to join the longpaws or wear a collar ever again. But we should make sure the ones in the town know that the Growl is coming back. Otherwise they'll be killed. Whatever you think of the longpaws, it feels very wrong to leave them to that fate."

His words had a powerful effect on the other former Leashed Dogs. Martha padded to his side, and Bella raised her muzzle rebelliously. Sunshine looped anxious circles around them.

Sweet's jaw stiffened. *She's going to forbid them from going anywhere near the Endless Lake,* thought Lucky. He watched Bella. He knew how stubborn his litter-sister could be. They didn't need tensions in the Pack right now, with the Growl coming and the Fierce Dogs nearby.

Lucky spoke quickly, careful to keep his eyes low and submissive. "Alpha, if you allow it, I could lead a group of dogs to the town to try to warn the longpaws. They are clever creatures, but their instincts are poor—they won't be able to sense the Growl coming." He lowered his head farther and spoke to the ground. "I promise we won't waste time. We'll be safely back up the cliff before the Growl comes."

Lucky stood very still. He could feel Sweet's eyes bearing down on him. *She knows I can't possibly guess when the Growl will arrive— no dog can. There's a risk we won't make it back. But she must understand what this means to the Leashed Dogs. And she's not like the last dog we called "Alpha." She will care.*

He held his breath hopefully, feeling the anxiety of the Leashed Dogs.

Sweet sighed. "I think it's foolish, but I won't stop you."

Lucky raised his head and blinked at her, grateful. *Nothing like our old Alpha!* he thought.

Sweet looked at him sternly. "Be careful, Beta. And hurry!"

She turned to the other dogs. "Who's going with him to help the longpaws?"

"I will," said Martha in her deep, soft voice.

Bella's golden tail gave a wag. "Me too. It will be the last thing I do for the longpaws. After that, they can go their own ways, and we will go ours."

Mickey trotted up to her, his eyes sparkling. "We'll help them. It's the right thing to do. But we'll be quick," he assured Sweet.

Sunshine and Daisy skipped excitedly.

"We'll save the longpaws!" Sunshine yipped.

But Bruno sidled up to Moon and sat heavily. "I'm staying here. I'm a Pack Dog now. My longpaws abandoned me, and the ones in the town are strangers." His eyes were cold, and Lucky looked at the old dog in surprise. *He's telling the truth. He doesn't care about his longpaws anymore.*

To Lucky's surprise, Snap ran up to the Leashed Dogs who were preparing to leave for the Endless Lake.

"I'll come," she yipped.

Bella turned to her. "But you were always a Wild Dog."

"I want to be useful," she said, flicking her ear dismissively.

"Thank you," murmured Mickey, tenderly licking the small

dog's ear. She looked up at him with a softness in her eyes. Lucky cocked his head. *Mickey and Snap are mates! How could I have missed it?*

Lucky felt a tap on his leg and turned to see Beetle looking up at him with admiration. "I'll go!" he offered.

Moon sprang forward and grabbed her pup by the scruff. "Oh no, you won't!" she snarled. "Longpaws killed your Father-Dog. Let the Leashed Dogs get this misplaced loyalty out of their systems. We owe the longpaws *nothing*."

Sweet cleared her throat, and the other dogs turned to look at her. "All the dogs who are staying behind—we need to be ready when the Growl comes. We should catch more prey, as we may struggle to find much in the aftermath of the Growl. Bruno and Moon, see what you can find around camp, but don't stray far. Every dog should keep a lookout for the Fierce Dogs, in case they make an appearance."

Bruno and Moon gave stiff nods and started jogging deeper into the valley, sniffing the freezing grass. Moon paused, turning to shoot Beetle a warning glance. The pup dipped his head and backed away from Lucky.

Sweet turned to the dogs who were preparing to leave for the town. "Don't forget what I said—I need you to be quick." She walked alongside Lucky, leading the group to the edge of the cliff. Bella and Martha led the way down, scaling the jagged rocks along the cliff face. Lucky hung back at Sweet's side. Her muzzle was close to his ear, and her voice became a whisper. "Be careful. Come back at the first sign of trouble." She rested her face alongside his. Lucky's heart ached as he breathed in her sweet scent. "Hurry back to me, my Beta," she said softly, before pulling away.

Lucky started along the cliff path, then looked back. Sweet was standing alone at the top of the cliff, a look of sorrow on her face.

Lucky tore his eyes away, hurrying after the other dogs. He promised himself he would see her again. But as he scrambled down the rocky incline, his belly was tight with tension and his whiskers prickled with sadness.

CHAPTER NINE

Lucky scurried down the rocks, hurrying to catch up with the other dogs as they picked their way around the cliff face. The air grew saltier as the wind glided over the Endless Lake, and a tingle of anxiety ran through Lucky's limbs. A sense of dread caught him at the back of the throat, and he cast his eyes to the top of the cliff. He could no longer see the grassy valley or the trees by the pond where they'd made their camp. He could no longer smell his Alpha's scent on the air.

His eyes trailed over the scrub farther along the cliffs, where it curved away from the lake. The Fierce Dogs' new lair was up there, hidden in damp caves. There was no hint of them on the air, but was Blade watching him even now, concealed behind the scrub?

Lucky's head snapped back when he heard a sharp yip beneath him. Sunshine had been struggling on the rocks, gathering herself together and leaping down clumsily. She had landed on the side of her paw and stopped to lick the sore spot.

Mickey paused just ahead of her. "Are you okay? Do you need help?"

"I'm fine," said the little dog proudly. She picked herself up and sprang down to the next stone. Her paws skidded as she landed, sending a rain of pebbles across the narrow path and over the edge of the cliff.

Lucky watched her anxiously. He could hear the distant crash and hiss of the Endless Lake down below. For an instant, he pictured a bundle of dirty white fur hurtling over the edge of the cliff, and he winced.

"We could help," he said gently, eager not to offend her. "We could lift you over the steeper rocks. Remember when we ran from the black cloud, and some of the climb was pretty steep? Others had help too—like Whine. There's no shame in it."

"I'm *fine*, really," Sunshine insisted. "I don't need help getting down." She flashed Mickey and Lucky a grateful look, then added in a smaller voice, "But I may need it getting up."

Mickey reached up and licked her on the nose. "Of course." He stayed a short way in front of her, with Lucky just behind, as they made their way down the side of the cliff.

They trod the bank of the Endless Lake until the town came into view. Even from a distance, Lucky could see loudcages humming along some of the streets. Longpaws were milling about. *It's just as we thought. They have no idea of the danger they are in.*

The other dogs were already resting at the edge of the town, staying out of view, when Mickey, Sunshine, and Lucky joined them.

"Look!" yapped Bella. "The Lake-Dog is agitated. She *knows* something's about to happen."

Lucky looked at the lake with a shudder. His litter-sister was right. Its usual rhythm was broken. It bucked and twisted uncertainly.

It's just as I imagined it. The lake must have broken its banks when the Big Growl came—and it could do it again.

"I don't like it," whined Snap.

Mickey padded to her side and rested his muzzle against her cheek. "We won't stay long—will we, Beta?"

"We'll warn the longpaws and head back as quickly as possible," Lucky agreed. The fur rose along his back. Had something shifted in the earth beneath his paws?

It's just my imagination, he told himself—though he didn't quite believe that.

He led the way to the edge of the town where the dogs paused, watching the orange-furred longpaws go about their business. A couple were dragging sticks with bushy heads along the street, collecting piles of sand, broken clear-stone, and mess that had tumbled from spoil-boxes. They barked cheerfully to one another. A loudcage rumbled down the street, and another orange longpaw popped his head out and waved at them.

Lucky edged a little closer, gesturing with his tail for the other dogs to follow him. They clung close to the wall, keeping out of sight.

"What are those ones doing?" whispered Mickey.

Lucky looked beyond the longpaws with sticks to some others who were pushing long pieces of wood into the ground in a circle. "I don't know," Lucky murmured.

"They don't get it, do they?" said Snap. "Look at them. They haven't sensed a thing."

"They're not like us," Bella explained. "They don't have the Spirit Dogs to help them."

"So what do we do?" asked Snap. "How are we supposed to warn them?"

Lucky licked his lips, unsure.

Little Sunshine spoke up. "My longpaws always knew

something was wrong when I ran around in circles and yapped. Maybe we could try that?"

"We could lean against their legs and push them away from the Endless Lake," Martha suggested. "Maybe they'll get the idea."

Bella's ears pricked up. "My longpaws would have been alert to danger if I'd howled."

"All good ideas," agreed Lucky. He looked out over the bank of the Endless Lake. The water spun in strange circles, sending up flecks of white foam. Fear prickled his bones. "We have to act quickly. Do everything you can to let the longpaws know they're in danger—but don't let them capture you! Be prepared to flee on my word. We may need to run back to camp at a moment's notice."

"Yes, Beta," murmured the dogs.

"Good. Let's go to it!" Lucky bounded along the street. He heard the other dogs running after him. He looked back to see Sunshine skipping in erratic loops, yipping urgently. Snap and Daisy were imitating the Omega, prancing and spinning. Lucky slowed down, wondering how the longpaws would react.

At first they looked amused. The two carrying sticks stopped their sweeping and pointed. But when Bella and Lucky started howling, the longpaws tensed. Martha and Mickey ran to the two longpaws, but they backed away, forelegs raised defensively. They joined another longpaw to skirt around the long pieces of wood that had been pushed into the ground.

"Not that way!" barked Mickey in exasperation. "Run away from the Endless Lake!"

"You're scaring them!" Lucky called. "They don't understand." He looked beyond the pieces of wood and shuddered. There was a deep bite in the ground; it reminded Lucky of the cave bowl in the Fierce Dog's new lair.

"What's that noise?" barked Martha, her head swiveling around toward the lake.

Mickey slammed to a halt, his ears pricking up. "The Endless Lake is pulling away from its bank. Something terrible is about to happen!"

Fear gripped Lucky's belly, and his hackles rose instinctively. "We must get back to camp!" he barked.

"But the longpaws!" whined Mickey. "Maybe it's good that they're frightened of us! It could be enough." He dropped his head, growling, and advanced on the longpaws. Snap hurried to his side with a snarl in her throat.

Two of the longpaws dodged away, but the other backed toward the great hole in the ground. He wrenched free one of the long pieces of wood and waved it in the air. Snap hesitated, her forepaw raised, but Mickey started barking and stepped even closer to the longpaw, almost close enough to touch. "Leave! Go away!"

The longpaw howled in fear and slammed the wooden stick against Mickey's side. Mickey yelped in pain but didn't retreat. Lucky's ears flicked back and he stepped forward, prepared to drag the Farm Dog away to safety. As the longpaw raised the stick again, another longpaw shrieked. Everyone turned to see this longpaw pointing at the Endless Lake.

They've noticed that something is happening! thought Lucky. The water had pulled far back into the Endless Lake, as if massing itself into a huge wave. The longpaw picked up a small black box with a thin tail and barked into it in a panicked voice. Other longpaws began to run along the street, thrashing their arms wildly.

The air was filled with the sound of howling longpaws and growling loudcages.

Lucky raised his voice over the noise. "Dogs, the longpaws have seen the lake! They know they are in danger! We have to get out of here, *now*. Our Alpha is waiting. We must hurry back to camp!"

"I'm coming, Lucky!" Mickey barked back, spinning around.

The longpaw holding the stick flinched away from him, one

orange hind paw slipping over the edge of the hole. He yipped in panic, dropping the piece of wood. His forepaws flailed, and he reached forward, but there was nothing to grab onto. With a terrified shriek, the longpaw fell backward into the pit.

CHAPTER TEN

Lucky and the other dogs ran to Mickey's side to peer over the edge of the pit. The longpaw had fallen several dog-lengths down to the bottom—too deep for him to climb out. Orange forepaws flailed against the earth. He cried out, but his shrill voice was lost in the din and screech of loudcages and barking longpaws.

The Farm Dog pawed at the edge of the pit. "We have to help him!"

"No, Mickey!" Lucky growled, determined to drag his Pack-mate away from danger. "He isn't our responsibility. Let the longpaws help their own!"

"Lucky's right," agreed Snap. "That longpaw struck you. He isn't your friend."

Mickey was more forgiving. "He was scared! He thought I was going to hurt him."

Bella touched her nose against the Farm Dog's shoulder. "Let his own Pack save him. We should be getting back to camp."

"But they don't know he's in danger! Didn't you see the Endless Lake? It's rising over its banks. It will come here. It will drown him." Mickey's eyes were wild with fear. "No one will save him. He'll die alone!" he whined sorrowfully.

Lucky looked out at the chaos on the street. Longpaws were running toward loudcages, scrambling inside before the beasts pulled away. He couldn't get a clear view of the lake from here, but he feared Mickey was right. Earth-Dog's tremors would whip it up, driving Lake-Dog over the bank.

Lucky's ears flicked back. Overhead, there was a distant murmur—a sound he had heard before, though it took him a moment to place it. It was the hum of the giant birds, with clear-stone bodies as large as loudcages and whirring wings the length of longpaw houses. Already the ground was shivering, from the birds or the Growl, Lucky couldn't be sure. It sent cascades of soil tumbling from the walls of the pit onto the longpaw's orange head. The longpaw slipped down onto all fours, shaking away the soil.

Lucky looked back across the street. Mickey was right. The longpaws were barking anxiously, leaving in loudcages or running toward the loudbirds, which were swooping over the street, probably searching for somewhere to land. No one would notice that the fallen longpaw was missing.

Lucky turned back to the pit. The longpaw outstretched his orange forelegs and whimpered.

Tightness gathered in Lucky's chest. *He won't be drowned. He'll be buried alive. . . .*

With a sickening lurch, Lucky remembered being trapped in the rock bowl, deep within the Fierce Dog's lair. His fur rose along his back as he pictured the high walls. He recalled the airlessness and the knowledge that he couldn't get out. Fear clutched at his chest. *I promised Sweet we'd run at the first sign of trouble.* Why was he hesitating?

"Please," Mickey whimpered. "We can't abandon him."

Pity weighed heavily on Lucky and he hesitated, throwing fretful looks over his shoulder, casting about for an object, something that could help. He shook his head. Against his better judgment, he found himself saying, "Get one of those wooden sticks. We'll try to get him out."

Mickey's tail wagged with relief as he grabbed a stick and dragged it to the edge of the pit. Bella threw Lucky a reproachful look but bent to help to lift the piece of wood with her mouth.

Together, the three dogs lowered it down to the longpaw.

Sunshine was hopping anxiously. "The air feels strange! It's strange!" she yipped.

Lucky's ears swiveled back. She was right, something was happening. "Hurry, everyone," he muttered, his voice muffled by the piece of wood that he clutched in his jaws.

Mickey steered the stick down into the pit, pushing at it with his paws. At first the longpaw hesitated. Then he reached out his forepaws and tried to grip the end of the stick.

The ground bucked violently, and the sound of tearing hardstone filled the air.

"The Growl!" cried Bella.

The wooden stick slipped from the dogs' grip and fell into the pit, narrowly avoiding the cowering longpaw. Lucky's ears flicked down, and he gasped as he looked back at the street. The gray hardstone was splitting in two and wet earth was bursting up between it, twisting and bubbling. The smell of the Endless Lake rose on the air. It was everywhere—around them, above them, even beneath them. The ground trembled and a nearby spoil-box tumbled onto its side, bouncing along the street.

Fear screamed in Lucky's ears, and for a moment he froze with panic. Martha was trembling, Sunshine was a cringing ball of fur, and Bella and Snap were scrambling against each other, trying to run in the confusion.

Only Mickey was still trying to rescue the longpaw. He was tugging at another plank that had sunk at an angle in the trembling ground. He yanked and pulled, easing it free.

Every instinct begged Lucky to run, but he bit down his terror and rushed to Mickey's aid. Together, they started dragging the piece of wood toward the pit. Snapping out of her panic, Martha came to help them. The powerful water-dog was able to lift the plank over the edge of the pit.

The loudbirds had arrived and were hovering over the town. They threw down long furs, and the terrifying yellow-furred longpaws scrambled out to the ground as Lucky had seen them do in the forest. But these longpaws weren't interested in the dogs—they scarcely looked at Lucky and the others as they landed on the street, rushing to round up their own kind.

"They've forgotten about this one," murmured Mickey as he steered the stick down into the pit, panting with the effort.

The orange longpaw was already half-buried with soil. He scrambled wildly, unable to free himself to reach the stick. Lucky's heart raced. *He isn't going to make it . . . none of us are!*

Then he heard Martha's deep voice behind him. "The Lake-Dog is coming, but she will wait until we have left. She is the River-Dog's litter-sister. I sent her my thoughts, and I know she has listened."

Lucky didn't know if he believed her, but Martha's words reassured him and gave him strength. Sucking in his breath, he helped Mickey angle the stick as Martha lowered it as far as she could.

The ground lurched, sending the longpaw flying. He threw up his paws and grasped the end of the plank. The ground shook and Lucky braced his legs, trying not to stumble as he and the other dogs backed up carefully, heaving the longpaw up with the stick.

The air screeched beneath the wings of the giant birds as it was whipped into a blizzard of dirt and debris. Lucky could hardly open his eyes. His jaw throbbed as he pulled backward. When he risked a glimpse into the swirling air, he was relieved to see the longpaw reaching his paws over the edge of the pit and scrambling up the stick onto the ground. He rolled onto his side, stunned and panting for breath.

Lucky looked around. The last of the orange longpaws were scrambling up the strips of fur into the bellies of the giant birds. Lucky shouted to Mickey over the noise, "If he doesn't go now, they'll leave without him!"

Mickey was quick to understand. He rushed to the long-paw's side and licked his rough orange fur to revive him. Then he started to head-butt the exhausted longpaw, whining as loudly as he could.

The longpaw no longer seemed to be afraid of Mickey. He rose to a sitting position and reached for the Farm Dog, resting an orange paw across his head.

Mickey whined louder and the longpaw looked around, then seemed to come to his senses. Stumbling onto his hind legs, he started to run with lurching steps, making for the last of the giant birds, which was lifting itself into the sky.

I guess that's all poor Mickey gets for gratitude, thought Lucky bitterly. *A pat on the head for saving his life.*

But as the longpaw reached the strip of fur dangling from the giant bird, he turned around. He stared at the dogs, then reached out his foreleg, barking and beckoning to Mickey. It was clearly an offer.

Snap whined, her tail between her legs.

Lucky felt a whine rising in his throat. *He'll go with the longpaw! It's all he's ever wanted.*

Mickey's tail thrashed, and he panted at the longpaw. Then he turned and ran back to the other dogs. He didn't even watch as the longpaw climbed the strip of fur and was helped by others into the belly of the bird, which then rose into the air and flew away toward the forest and far into the distance.

Lucky was astonished. "You've always wanted to be with long-paws, and now, when you had a chance to go with them, you didn't take it!"

"He wasn't *my* longpaw," Mickey barked. "And anyway, things have changed. I'm not the same dog that I used to be. I don't belong with longpaws anymore. I belong with my Pack."

Lucky panted happily. *They've all come such a long way,* he thought, bursting with pride. Not even Sunshine was watching the retreating loudbirds as they disappeared with their bellies full of longpaws. Lucky felt a warm flush of affection for all these dogs, who had once resisted losing their leashes and had mourned for so long for their lives before the Big Growl.

The Growl!

Lucky came to his senses. This was no time to relax. The earth was shaking harder, and water was fizzing and spluttering from the yawning gaps in the hardstone street. He cast a wary eye toward the Endless Lake. The water was lifting and bucking furiously, rising in the distance and channeling toward land with great speed.

"It's time to go!" he barked.

As the dogs turned toward the banks of the lake and the jagged path to their camp, a deep rumbling rose from the cliff. They watched, ears pricked and bodies tense, as rocks started tumbling from the cliff face.

"Our path home!" barked Mickey, wild-eyed.

Lucky's pulse raced in his ears. "The rest of the Pack is up there!" he yelped.

The jutting edge of the cliff gave a furious growl and collapsed into the lake.

CHAPTER ELEVEN

Lucky stared at the swirling clouds of dust and dirt that floated around the broken cliff. His heart throbbed with tension. He could think of only one thing: *Sweet!* She was up there, on the cliff, with the rest of their Pack. Were they far enough from the cliff face? Were they safe?

"The lake!" barked Bella.

The dogs spun around to see the bubbling, frantic waters. The giant white wave was charging toward the bank, building every moment, sucking the water nearby into itself. At first it was the size of a loudcage, then a loudbird, then a longpaw house.

"Lake-Dog is eating all the water in her path!" Bella whined. "She's so hungry, she'll swallow the town!"

"Run!" Lucky howled, dashing toward the base of the cliffs. The cracked hardstone was splitting along the length of the street, and salt water burst out, showering Lucky as he ran. The ground bucked beneath him and he rolled onto his side, springing back onto his paws and then running toward the sandy bank of the Endless Lake.

To make it back to camp, they would need to run along the bank—to risk the Lake-Dog's wrath. He turned to glance at the other dogs, who were bounding behind him. Martha's lips were moving. Was she sending her thoughts to the Lake-Dog, begging her to be merciful, to hold down her rage a little longer?

Lucky turned back toward the cliffs. Part of the cliff face had fallen, revealing sharp gray rock. Roots and debris dangled off the exposed edge, and clouds of soil billowed around it, darkening the sky.

"We can't go anywhere near *that!*" Bella barked. "It isn't safe."

Mickey caught up, staring out over the water. "We'll have to risk running farther along the bank of the lake—there must be another way up the cliffs."

"But the water is coming!" yipped Daisy, shaking with fear.

Lucky thought furiously. The huge white wave seemed to be quickening to the shore, just as it was growing larger. How far would they make it along the bank before it reached them?

"We have to go *now!*" barked Mickey.

Lucky gave a stiff nod. "Everyone, this way!" He lurched along the bank of the lake, scarcely daring to look out at the pummeling water and the deadly wave that was gathering force. The dogs scrambled on the trembling sand, their legs pulsing and their breath heaving. They skirted around the cliff, away from the broken cliff face. The rocks rose sharply, impossible to climb. *It's a mistake! We should have risked the broken cliff—we can't get away—we'll be drowned by the wave!* Just as panic seized him, Lucky spotted a path through the rocks that seemed to wind upward through tangles of grass.

Thank the Forest-Dog!

"This way!" he barked, scrambling up the incline. Bella, Snap, and Mickey were right behind him. He turned to check on the others. Daisy was working hard, charging up the rock ridge on her short legs. Martha followed her, carrying Sunshine by her scruff like a puppy. *Of course, poor Sunshine!* In the panic, he had forgotten the little Omega. How lucky they were that Martha was with them. Affection and gratitude coursed through Lucky's limbs.

The path along the edge of the cliffs wound deeper, taking the dogs away from the lake. Soon it plateaued, making it easier to climb. But Lucky was still on edge. High walls of rock surrounded them and the ground was quivering, though not as badly as it had on the beach. *But if the rocks start to collapse, we'll be buried alive!* His tail shot to his flank, and he tried to push the thought away.

Lucky's mind returned to the dogs they'd left behind. He thought of Moon and her pups, Storm, Bruno, even Whine. Most of all, he pictured Sweet. He threw himself forward with all his might, charging along the path up the cliff. His muscles burned, and he fought for breath. *What if something's happened to her? What if our good-bye on the cliff top was the last I'll ever see of her?*

He heard a thunder of paws, and Bella appeared at his side. "They'll be okay," she murmured.

He glanced at her anxiously and didn't answer.

As they reached the top of the cliff, they could see over the jagged rocks down to the Endless Lake. The enormous white wave had overrun the streets of the town, gobbling up houses and sweeping abandoned loudcages into its belly. Lucky shivered with terror. *That was almost us.*

It was disorienting to reach the top of the cliffs. They had arrived at a different point from the one they were used to, but even so it was clear that everything had changed. Part of the slope had collapsed. Lucky's eyes trailed over a deep crater of rock and earth mounds, where an upside-down tree jutted out at an angle, clods of soil dangling from its roots.

The dogs padded warily over the churned-up grass, struggling to get their bearings in such an altered world.

Lucky realized that the ground was no longer shaking beneath his paws. *The Growl has passed. At least it wasn't as bad as last time. The Pack may be okay, if they stayed clear of the cliffs.*

"There are the trees and the pond," whined Sunshine.

The little dog was right—the pond was just up ahead, though Lucky could hardly recognize it. Several of the trees had fallen, and silt-filled water pooled around their trunks. Most of the long grass had been flattened. But it was worse toward the edge of the cliff, which was now much more rugged and ended abruptly at a sheer drop.

The Pack had vanished. Although the Endless Lake still crashed in the distance, an eerie silence fell over the valley. Lucky barked sharply, then barked again, listening for a reply, but none came.

Lucky's trembling legs gave way beneath him, and he slumped onto the ground like one of the fallen trees. *Sweet . . .* He should never have left her to go to the town, not when he sensed danger. Unbearable anguish swept through him.

Sunshine was the first to start whimpering. Soon Mickey, Snap, and Bella were whining and yelping. Then Martha threw back her black head and howled.

"Listen!" yapped Daisy, cutting over the frantic dogs. "Can you hear something?"

The others fell silent, and Lucky's ears pricked up. Someone was barking in the distance, on the far side of the pond!

Daisy burst forward, her tail wagging frenziedly.

"Wait!" ordered Lucky. "We have to be careful. The Growl has moved things about. Take it slowly and keep away from the trees; they could be unstable." He led the way over the curving landscape, careful to test the ground before setting down his paw. But inside, he was just as desperate as Daisy to run to the sound. Hope burned in his chest.

As they skirted around the pond, the yaps grew louder.

"I can hear Storm!" yelped Martha, her tail thumping.

"And Bruno!" added Sunshine.

"Where are you?" barked Lucky.

"Over here!" Bruno barked back. "Under a tree trunk at the edge of the pond."

Lucky sniffed along the ground until he could scent his Pack-mates. All at once, he saw them. They were sheltering amid the knotted roots of a fallen tree. The trunk had fallen into the pond itself and was half-submerged under water. Lucky dipped his head to peer beneath, and a series of snouts greeted him. Among them, Lucky spotted Sweet's pale muzzle, and he panted with relief.

"We rushed under here when the trees began to fall," she explained. "The roots protected us. But then the ground shook again, and the tree rolled, trapping us. We were waiting for things to feel calm again before we dared to start digging our way out."

Mickey sprang down to the side of the tree. "The Growl seems to have passed now. We'll help you." The Farm Dog started kicking away the sodden earth and Snap hurried to help him, digging easily with her short, powerful legs. Daisy helped Mickey and Snap by pushing back the dirt, and Lucky, Bella, and Martha cleared a path while Sunshine yipped encouragement.

"You're nearly there!" shouted the little Omega.

A moment later, Beetle scrambled out from under the tree trunk. "Lucky!" he yapped. His thin tail lashed the air, and he bounded around his Packmates ecstatically. "Don't you think that was a clever place to hide from the Growl?"

"It certainly was," said Lucky, his tail wagging with delight.

"It was all my idea!" the young dog said proudly.

"That's true," said Thorn, following her litter-brother out onto the wet grass and shaking out her fur. "He said it would be the perfect shelter—that this big tree would stop other trees from hurting us if they fell down. And Sweet agreed!"

"Yes, I did." Two lean forelegs reached through the gap beneath the tree, and Sweet shook herself free. Lucky rushed to her side, growling gently with excitement.

"You were clever to avoid the cliffs."

"What happened?" Her dark eyes met his.

"Part fell into the Endless Lake. But we're all okay. We saved the longpaws by warning them of the danger—they escaped into those giant birds."

Sweet tilted her head. "We saw them high overhead, but there was so much chaos we didn't know what they were."

"The Leashed Dogs worked quickly," Lucky told her. "They proved their loyalty to the Pack, especially Mickey." Lucky thought better than to say more about what had happened—Sweet probably wouldn't understand Mickey's insistence on saving the longpaw from the pit. Mickey's eyes glittered, and he dipped his black-and-white head.

"I am glad to hear it. We are all well too," said Sweet as the rest of the Pack shuffled out from under the tree trunk. Their pelts were wet and covered in soil and grass, but no dog was injured.

Sweet broke away from Lucky to pad farther into the valley. She gasped, glancing back. "It's unbelievable. I thought the cliffs were solid, like a mountain, but they fell apart when the Earth-Dog shook her fur." She started farther across the grass, but Moon called her back.

"Alpha, be careful! The ground could still move. It's better to stay away from the cliffs. We need you alive and well!"

Sweet turned and trotted back to the Pack. "You are wise," she murmured to Moon. Then she turned to nudge Beetle and Thorn. "Just like your pups." She ran her shrewd brown eyes over the Pack. "And we will need plenty of wisdom and intelligence in the days ahead."

Lucky watched the Pack too. The dogs who had emerged from the pond were licking the dirt from their coats and rolling in the grass to get clean, but their eyes stayed fixed on their Alpha. Storm was shaking out her short fur, her head cocked and her ears pricked.

Sweet looked out across the valley. "We will have to rebuild a camp, something that we can defend. Now is the time we need to stand together. The Growl returned, and we survived. If it has passed, it means the Fierce Dogs are also getting to their paws and shaking off the dirt and destruction. Blade knew about this Growl, she *saw* it. Now she'll be convinced that her prophecy is true—that Earth-Dog is angry and needs a sacrifice. She'll be coming for us soon, and we need to be ready."

Lucky lowered his muzzle, gazing out toward the cliffs. He didn't want to think about Blade and her disturbing visions, or how they strangely paralleled his own. But Sweet was right: The Growl would make Blade more determined than ever. She would come for Storm and any dog who tried to protect her.

Lucky shivered. *We don't have much time.*

CHAPTER TWELVE

The Pack turned to one another, heads cocked in confusion.

"What does the Growl have to do with Blade?" asked Moon.

Bruno sat heavily and cleared his throat. "She's right, you know, Alpha. You are very wise, and we all agree that Blade is a menace. But there are limits, even to her power. She cannot control the elements—no dog can!"

The dogs started barking in agreement, and Lucky realized that Sweet hadn't told the Pack what the four of them had heard Blade ranting about—how she was convinced of Earth-Dog's wrath, fervently believing that worse was to come unless the Spirit Dog was appeased by Storm's death.

The fur rose along Lucky's back. He padded up to Sweet and nudged her gently with his nose. "Are you sure you want to tell them?" he murmured. "They don't know about the dreams. It could scare them."

He heard a rasp and looked down to see Whine. The small dog's eyes bulged and his tongue hung out. "*What* could scare us?" he panted. "What don't you want us to know, Beta?" He turned to the Pack with a malevolent glare. "Our Alpha and Beta are keeping secrets from us. Always whispering to each other . . ."

A ripple of suspicious yaps ran through the Pack.

Sweet glared at the stumpy little dog and he shrank back, hiding between Bruno and Martha.

"It isn't like that," Lucky insisted.

Mickey looked at him thoughtfully. "Did Blade say something when you were trapped in her lair?"

Storm stiffened and gave a low growl.

Sweet sighed. "Mickey, you are clever. I didn't know how much to tell you all. Lucky's right; there's no point scaring you."

Moon's eyes widened. "If you want us to work together, we need to know what's going on."

Sweet reached out a pale paw and licked off some dirt. "It is probably for the best . . . if Lucky doesn't mind?"

Lucky drew in his breath, his tail flicking nervously to his side. He didn't like the idea of all the dogs knowing so much about his dreams. It made him feel exposed. *It isn't just about you,* he told himself sharply. Swallowing back his fear, he dipped his head in agreement. The Pack became quiet, waiting for Sweet to speak.

"Do you remember that night during the Great Howl, when Lucky collapsed?" she began. "He saw images during the Howl, and they overwhelmed him. . . ." Her voice softened. "There have been dreams, too."

There was a murmur from the assembled dogs, and Lucky sensed them stiffening, their ears pricking up and their tails straight behind them. He didn't want to look at them directly. He gazed at the distant, broken cliffs, unable to meet the curious looks of the other dogs. *What if they think I'm weak?* He turned back to watch Sweet from the corner of his eye.

"What sort of dreams?" whined Dart, her voice quivering.

Sweet lowered a slender paw. "He has seen a snowstorm, and a ferocious battle between Packs of dogs."

"The Storm of Dogs," murmured Snap, her ears flicking back. "Are you still dreaming about that, Lucky?"

"Like those horrible stories my Mother-Dog told me about long ago," whimpered Dart. "The Spirit Dogs turned on one another. Lightning fought the Sky-Dogs, Earth-Dog fought River-Dog, back in the Dawn of Time."

Snap crinkled her nose in concentration. "I remember something too . . . but wasn't it a fight between dogs, like Sweet said? A fight to the death, where only one Pack was left standing?"

Moon lifted her muzzle authoritatively. "Yes, a battle between Packs."

The sharp smell of fear-scent caught Lucky's nose. *So many of them have heard about the Storm of Dogs from the stories of their puppyhood. It scares them.*

"That's the trouble," said Sweet. "Most of us have heard of the Storm of Dogs, but we're not sure what it means. Lucky's dreams keep returning to it."

"They're just stories, aren't they?" asked Martha. "Tales that Mother-Dogs tell their pups to stop them being naughty. 'Don't fight, pups, the Spirit Dogs are watching. You don't want to bring on the Storm of Dogs.' That sort of thing."

"I thought so too," said Sweet. "But now I'm not so sure. . . . When Lucky was trapped with the Fierce Dogs, Blade told him something . . . something incredible."

Lucky risked a look around the Pack. The dogs were stiff with tension.

Sweet licked her lips. "Blade said that she had seen a vision of fighting dogs . . . and it matched the images Lucky had seen in his dreams."

There were gasps from the Pack. Sweet cleared her throat and went on.

"Lucky didn't share his visions with Blade. He stayed quiet, which was the right thing to do. Blade told him that Earth-Dog growled because she was angry, and that she will growl again and destroy the world. And that there is only one way to stop her."

No dog spoke. Their fear-scent still drifted on the air.

It was Storm who broke the silence. "This is because of me, isn't it? I always thought Blade killed Wiggle because she thought he was weak, and maybe she wanted us dead because she hated our Mother-Dog, some old fight or something. Then I thought she must be mad because I escaped her Pack. But everything you say . . . is *that* why she killed Fang? Why she wants to kill me? Because she thinks—" Storm's voice rose. "She thinks I'll cause the Storm of Dogs?"

Sweet hesitated, and Lucky finally spoke. "Yes, Storm. She believes that pups born to her Pack after the Big Growl will bring about the Storm of Dogs and the final Growl. That's why she killed Wiggle when she discovered you'd survived being abandoned. Fang only survived as long as he did because she was trying to use him to catch you."

Storm's muzzle wrinkled with sorrow at the mention of her littermates.

Mickey's whiskers flexed, and he gave a long whine. "And the pup . . . the one we found in the Dog-Garden?" He gave Storm a quick look.

"That was Blade's own pup," Lucky said quietly.

Sweet thumped the damp earth with her forepaw. "Which means she's serious. If she's prepared to kill her own pup to save herself or her Pack, or dogs in general—whatever it is she believes she's saving—she'll stop at nothing to kill Storm. That's why Blade captured Lucky—to get to Storm. We only escaped because Earth-Dog trembled. Once Blade thought she had Storm in her grasp, she killed Fang without any remorse. Whatever else you could say about him, he was loyal to her. No dog can deny that. I watched her tear that pup apart with my own eyes."

It was a while before any dog spoke.

Finally Moon crept forward, her black ears folded back. "If Blade's coming after us, we should run. She's even got our old Alpha on her side." The Farm Dog shuddered. "We're completely outnumbered, and we've lost enough Packmates already. We can't hope to fight all those Fierce Dogs. Running is our only option."

"Running where?" said Mickey. "She'll find us . . . you know she will."

"But we can't just stay here and wait for Blade to come. There are pups among us." Moon's eyes widened as she looked to Beetle and Thorn.

Thorn stamped a black forepaw on the grass. "We're not pups anymore. We can fight, just like Storm! She taught us how."

"No!" growled Moon. Her blue eyes flashed dangerously. "I'm not losing another pup!"

Lucky ran his tongue over his nose uncertainly. *Mickey's right. If we leave now, Blade will follow us. We'll never get away from her.* It was his litter-sister Bella who spoke next.

"I don't think we should run," she said firmly. "There are pups among us, and older dogs . . . and we can't run forever. Sooner or later, the Fierce Dogs would catch us. Better to confront them while we are well fed and rested than have them creep up on us."

"We won't slow any dog down!" Thorn protested, and the Pack burst into a series of barks, with some dogs siding with Moon and others with Mickey.

Whine squeezed forward and cleared his throat. "There is another way."

"Another way?" echoed Dart. "What's that, Whine?"

The dogs quieted down, waiting for the little black squash-faced dog to speak.

Whine panted, his pink tongue lolling from his mouth. "We can't fight Blade, and we can't run away. The solution is obvious: We give her what she wants."

Lucky and Mickey snarled with disgust, but Whine raised his voice to speak over it. "There's no point being all *honorable* about an attack-dog—as the Sun-Dog rises and sets, she's a Fierce Dog and always will be. She's violent and untrustworthy. She wasn't born to the Pack, and no Pack Dog should die protecting her. We don't owe her anything."

Lucky bristled with rage. *How dare Whine accuse Storm of being untrustworthy when he's the nastiest, sneakiest dog around?* He expected protests from the Pack, but some of them had grown silent again, considering the small dog's words. Snap's head was cocked, her ears lowered. Moon gnawed absently at a forepaw.

Lucky looked to Storm, worried she would launch an attack on Whine. But instead of rising to anger, she had lowered her head sadly. She huddled into herself, looking more like a lost puppy than a ferocious attack-dog.

Whine carried on, unapologetic. "We've worked so hard to

avoid the Fierce Dogs. Who can say how far we've walked? They always find us, wherever we are. Should we really be risking our lives for an outsider?" His eyes bulged as they shifted between the dogs, and his voice became louder and shrill with excitement. "And what if Blade is right—her visions don't sound so different from Lucky's, and we believed *him*."

Something snapped inside Lucky, and he sprang at the stout little dog, throwing him onto the ground and pinning him down by the throat with a furious growl. "How dare you! Storm has proven her loyalty many times over, while you . . . you have shown how quick you are to judge, and to betray. No dog with a shred of honor would suggest such a thing! I should march you over the cliff right now to teach you a lesson, you rotten little rat!"

Whine trembled beneath Lucky's grip. "It was just an idea!" he spluttered.

"Beta," said Sweet gently. "It's a filthy idea, and typical of Whine's cowardice—but he's allowed to express it."

Reluctantly Lucky pulled back, and Whine scuttled to cower behind Bruno.

"We can't even think about handing Storm over like that," said Martha, padding to the young Fierce Dog's side. "Storm has always shown her dedication to the Pack, even fighting her way back to us when Blade captured her. And she didn't give in during the Trial of Rage—she fought her litter-brother fairly and proved that she could rise above her former Pack." Martha licked Storm's ears tenderly. "We are fortunate to have her."

Storm pressed against Martha, burying her muzzle in the great dog's shaggy black coat. Lucky felt affection spring from his fur. There had been a coldness between the two dogs for a while after they had fought about whether to confront the Fierce Dogs, but the rift had healed.

Moon spoke from the other side of the circle of dogs. "Storm risked her life to rescue Fiery. I know we couldn't save him in the end, but that wasn't her fault . . . it wasn't any dog's fault."

"She tried to help our Father-Dog!" yipped Thorn.

"She's part of the Pack," Beetle added.

Daisy spoke up too. "I can't imagine it here without her . . . we're not going to just give her over to the Fierce Dogs, are we? That wouldn't be true to our dog-spirits. We aren't foxes or sharp-claws!"

Lucky cast his eyes around the Pack. Some of the dogs who hadn't spoken looked pensive and uneasy. He noticed that Dart was gazing out toward the broken cliffs, and Bruno wouldn't meet his eye.

Whine shuffled forward, apparently unscathed by his brief tussle with Lucky. He pressed one forepaw into the mud beside the pond and raised his gaze to meet Lucky's, his eyes bulging. "Do you recognize your own idea?" he taunted. "The rule of Four Paws. If three other dogs join me, they'll be voting for turning Storm over to the Fierce Dogs and freeing ourselves from this terrible threat forever. They'll be voting for a new time of peace—no more running, no more fights. The other dogs would have to listen to us—why, it's our Beta's own rules."

Sweet rose to her full height, and Whine flinched but kept his paw firmly pressed in the mud.

"Should I remind you that *I'm* your Alpha?" she snarled. "*You* don't get to make decisions."

"Of course you are, and we respect you," he panted, dipping his head in an insincere show of deference. "But is our new Alpha afraid to hear the counsel of her Pack? Would you undermine your own Beta by ignoring his *brilliant* means for coming to decisions?"

The swift-dog wrinkled her muzzle, her ears twitching pensively.

Don't allow it, Sweet, Lucky silently willed. *Ignore the cunning little rat—it isn't fair to Storm!* He knew better than to speak out at this stage—it was important for Sweet to show her strength as a decision maker in front of her Pack. They all waited as she took a step forward and looked about.

Sweet took a deep breath. "Very well," she said coolly. "You can have your vote. If any other dog wishes to abandon their Packmate, let him or her speak now."

CHAPTER THIRTEEN

Lucky could feel the tension bearing down on him. The air was so silent that he could hear the wind rippling over the pond and an insect buzz toward the valley. Then Dart stepped forward on her skinny legs, hesitated, and pressed a paw next to Whine's.

Lucky smarted, grinding his teeth.

"I'm sorry, Beta," murmured the chase-dog. "But I've never believed that a Fierce Dog belongs with us. It's nothing personal, she's just . . . different. She should be with her own Pack. Let them decide her future."

Lucky suppressed a growl of disgust. He was about to speak when he heard a heavy footfall and looked across the circle of dogs to see Bruno moving forward. The old dog ran a tongue over his dark muzzle before thumping his paw down next to Dart's.

SURVIVORS: STORM OF DOGS

"Storm is a member of *our* Pack!" Lucky barked, feeling betrayed.

Bruno gave a long sigh. "I'm sorry, Lucky. I don't want to turn the pup over to be killed. But sometimes tough decisions need to be made for the greater good. If Storm's departure means that Blade leaves us alone, or if there's a chance that it stops this 'Storm of Dogs,' then it's the right thing to do for the greater good." He sniffed, looking shamefaced despite his words. "We need to drive Storm out of the Pack now, before it's too late—let her take the chase with her."

Lucky growled and hurried to Storm's side, pressing close to her so that the young dog was flanked by him and Martha. He lowered his head and raised his haunches. Martha did the same, her top lip curling to reveal a row of white teeth. They glared at the rest of the Pack. The message was clear. *Any dog who wants to force Storm out will have to go through us.*

Silence fell over the Pack. Whine, Dart, and Bruno stayed where they were, their paws in the mud, as Lucky threw his challenging gaze on the other dogs. It would take only one more to pass a decision according to his own Four Paws method. *I don't care if I came up with Four Paws. I'm not letting any dog push Storm out of the Pack!* He held his breath, and time seemed to still. Then he heard the scuffle of a paw, and his heart lurched in his chest. Someone was coming forward! With a wince of surprise, he saw it was Sweet.

The swift-dog stepped in front of Whine and stopped. "Enough!" she snapped. "I have heard the counsel of my Pack, and I see that even among so many of us there is little appetite for your dishonorable plan—most of the dogs agree with my decision. Storm stays with us, and we will defend her."

Relief washed over Lucky, and for a moment he felt giddy with gratitude. *Of course Sweet would never let me down.*

Martha gave a rumbling bark of approval, and Storm's tail flicked briefly. Whine slunk away and Dart shrank back. Bruno shook his head and went to sit a short distance from the others, licking the mud from his forepaw. Lucky sighed, his eyes trailing over the assembled dogs. Moon blinked, resting her head on Beetle's brow. Snap leaned against Mickey's flank. *Most of the dogs look happier,* he realized. *Sweet's leadership has made them more at ease.*

"What will we do?" asked Snap. "We know Blade will come for Storm, and it won't take her long. She'll take the recent Growl as a sign of Earth-Dog's anger."

It was Bella who spoke up. "Until now, we've either run away or hidden deep within camp—we've let Blade make all the decisions, and we've stayed on the back paw."

"What do you suggest?" Sweet asked her.

Lucky watched curiously. Bella's eyes were sparkling, just as they had as a pup when she was up to something. "We need to catch Blade unawares. I have a plan." She looked about the Pack. "We will offer Blade a deal: The Fierce Dog Alpha can fight a battle for Storm's life, by the frozen river—but it will be a straight fight between Storm and Blade, and Blade must come alone."

A growl rumbled in Storm's throat. "I would gladly fight her. For my litter-brothers . . . for my Pack." She raised her muzzle proudly.

Lucky's body tensed, and he turned to her. "But you only came into your adult name recently, and Blade's much larger than you—and more experienced." He looked to Bella. "Anyway, I doubt Blade would play fair. Her whole Pack would come with her." His whiskers flexed. There was a new dampness in the air. Gray clouds were grouping overhead, and a cold drop of rain fell on Lucky's nose.

"Beta's right." Sweet nodded. "Blade won't come alone."

Bella's tail gave a triumphant wag. "Of course she won't! Lucky, do you remember the place we passed when we were following the Wild Pack's trail toward the Endless Lake? Where the grass began to disappear and the ground became sandy? There was a place on the riverbank where we found ourselves on a thin path between the river on one side and tall rocks on the other."

Moon cocked her head. "I know where you mean. The point where the air was getting salty, before we actually caught sight of the Endless Lake? It was a horrible place—so windy and remote."

Lucky remembered it too, though only vaguely. "It's quite a distance from here."

"Less than a day's walk," Bella replied. "And wouldn't it make a good spot for an ambush? We could tell Blade to meet Storm there, then hide behind the rocks and attack when the Fierce Dogs pass below. We would be coming from above and have the advantage. If we can isolate the leaders . . . What are Blade's deputies' names?"

Lucky remembered the two muscular Fierce Dogs who were always at their Alpha's side. "Mace and Dagger," he spat.

"That's right." Bella thumped down her paw. "If we can isolate them—"

"I've had enough of this!" Whine interrupted. "This is the stupidest plan I've ever heard. Everything would have been fine if you'd just pushed Storm out of the Pack. She's never belonged here." He glared at Sweet defiantly. "If you insist on fighting for Storm's life, I'm leaving. I'm not sticking around to be slaughtered by Fierce Dogs!"

Sweet's muzzle curled with distaste. "You always were a little coward," she snarled. "All you do is complain, and you're sly. . . . If you want to leave, be my guest. Go now!" She threw a challenging glare at the rest of the Pack. "That goes for any other dog who wants to go. You won't be forced to stay." Her gaze lingered on Dart and Bruno.

Bruno raised his eyes to look back at her, his bushy tail sinking between his legs. "I was worried about keeping Storm in the Pack—worried about what it meant for the other dogs—but you have made a decision, and you are our Alpha. I respect that decision. This is my Pack. I don't want to leave."

"Neither do I," whined Dart, shuffling nervously.

"And you don't have to," said Sweet. "As long as you are loyal, you have a home here."

Whine growled, showing his teeth. "How cozy," he sneered. "I'm sure you will all be very happy together. Until the Fierce Dogs get you, that is! Good-bye, foolish dogs. I guess I'm the only one clever enough to choose survival." He held his head high as he turned and walked away. The pouring rain grew heavier, turning into sheets of white sleet and Lucky watched until the small, stocky figure could no longer be seen in the haze.

He's the fool, Lucky thought with a pang of sadness. *He never was much of a hunter, and for all his venom he couldn't beat an injured sharpclaw kit in a fight.* After everything that Whine had done, Lucky knew he should be pleased that the little dog had left. *He's always been divisive. He tried to undermine me and stir up trouble from the moment I joined the Wild Pack.* But Lucky's ears fell low and his tail was listless beneath the hammering sleet. There was no anger in his heart. He doubted the little dog could survive on his own, or that he'd ever see him again.

CHAPTER FOURTEEN

The Pack huddled beneath the trees that were still standing, a short distance from the pond. The leafless branches offered little cover from the sleet. Sunshine shivered, crouching against Lucky's side.

"Where is the Sun-Dog? It's already dark, and it can't be nosun yet. " She shook her dirty white coat. "Do you think the Growl scared him away? The Sky-Dogs seem so angry these days," she whined.

Lucky didn't know what to say. Sunshine was right—the thick pelt of cloud was darkening, and the sleet was growing more persistent.

Bruno sighed. "He wasn't much of a fighter, but I'm still sorry to see Whine go. Losing any dog makes our Pack weaker." His sad brown eyes turned to Bella and Sweet. "Do you really think we can overcome the Fierce Dogs, even if we catch them unawares?

They've been raised to fight—it's in their blood. We've lost strong dogs, like Fiery, and our former Alpha is with them now. How can we hope to beat them?"

Bella was quiet for a moment, then perked up. "Perhaps we aren't a match for Blade's Pack *right now*. But we would be, if we had a few more dogs."

Snap cocked her head curiously. "Dogs don't grow on trees, you know. I can't think of the last time I saw any who weren't in our Pack and weren't Fierce Dogs."

"I can," said Bella with a proud lash of her tail. "Twitch's Pack! Remember how we told you that we saw them in the woods? They're a good group of dogs now that their crazy leader is dead, and they're strong fighters. If we can persuade them to help us, we'll have enough dogs between us to overwhelm the Fierce Dogs, particularly as we'll have the element of surprise."

Standing beneath a grizzled old tree, Sweet narrowed her eyes. "It isn't exactly an *honorable* plan. As I recall, you and your Leashed friends used the same sort of trickery when you attacked this Pack in our old territory, only that time you used foxes to bolster your numbers."

Bella's tail drooped, but she held her head high and returned Sweet's gaze. "That was a stupid mistake, and I would never repeat it. This time we'd have better, more trustworthy allies than foxes."

"What makes you so sure that those dogs are trustworthy?" asked Daisy. "We don't really know them, and they were aggressive when Terror was in charge."

"But he's not in charge anymore," Bella pointed out.

Dart trod nervously next to Bruno. "We can trust them. Twitch is their Alpha now, and he used to be one of us. He's Spring's litter-brother, after all," she said with a sad whine. "He's always been strong and brave. If he agrees to fight alongside us, he won't let us down."

Lucky winced, remembering Spring, the floppy-eared dog who had fought the Fierce Dogs so courageously down by the tall, striped building by the Endless Lake—what had the Fierce Dogs called it? The "lighthouse." He shivered, remembering the terrifying battle in the fog. Spring hadn't made it. The memory of her death returned to him, cutting sharply beneath his fur. He pictured the hunt-dog drifting on the current, farther and farther from land. One of her long ears had bobbed on the surface. The other had curved over her eye, as though in sleep. Lucky shook his head, pushing the image away.

Sweet rose to her paws, her eyes fixed on Bella. "A dishonorable plan, but it might just work."

Bella's tail was wagging. "I can go and find Twitch and his Pack to talk to them. Maybe one of the others could come with me. Mickey or Daisy?"

"No." Sweet stepped out into the sleet, her ears low. "We should all go. A divided Pack is too vulnerable, and we don't know what Blade will do next or when she will strike. We need to stick together."

Sunshine's eyes widened. "But the Sky-Dogs won't let us! It's so wet, and the Growl must have churned up the earth. Won't it be dangerous?"

"We'll be careful," Sweet told her. "And at least this weather may keep the Fierce Dogs away for a little longer. We should take advantage of it."

She started to walk tentatively down the slope, and Lucky hurried to her side. Water rolled down his sodden fur and lashed the soft earth. His paws skidded uncomfortably on mud, and he wondered if Sunshine was right to worry. *We don't really know how firm the land is beneath our paws. What if more of the cliffs fall away?* He shuddered, glancing back at the little Omega. Her face had set in a look of determination as she shuffled under the lashing downpour. Already her paws were caked in mud, and she moved unsteadily.

Lucky thought of the long route down to the river and beyond that, to Twitch's forest. This wasn't going to be easy.

Sweet led the Pack down the valley, careful not to come too close to the cliffs. Lucky guided her to the passage that cut along the lake, which he, Snap, and the others had used to escape the great wave and the wrecked town. *What if the Lake-Dog is still angry? What if she sends another wave to catch us?* Lucky didn't have the heart to share these concerns, but his eyes watched through the sleet, scanning the white-tipped tide, as the lake came dimly into view. It was hard to see much in the fading light, with wet snow seeping from the sky to meld with the salt waters below.

Descending the rocks was harder than climbing them, especially in these conditions. Lucky's paws slipped on the hardstone, and he struggled to get a proper hold. The sleet was freezing into patches of ice, invisible and deadly.

"Be extra careful here, it's really slippery!" Lucky barked back.

His warning came too late as Sunshine skidded on the ice, tumbled past Lucky, and thumped down hard on the slab in front of her. She gave a sharp yelp, and Lucky crouched down by her side.

"Are you okay? Are you hurt?"

With a wince, she rolled onto her paws. "I don't think so.

More shock than pain. I'll be okay in a moment."

Bruno nosed her gently with his whiskery muzzle. "Let me carry you."

"Thank you," Sunshine murmured. She sat still, clearly gathering as much dignity as she could muster, as Bruno gripped her scruff and scooped her up.

While it was hard to see the movement of the Endless Lake in the dying light, Lucky could hear that it had settled since the Growl. He looked out for giant waves as the Pack made the difficult descent onto the bank, but if anything, the water had pulled away from the land. With a shudder, Lucky remembered that it had a habit of retreating and surging back again. It had happened the night that he and Fiery's rescue party had hidden in a cave on the sand. They had awoken hours deep into no-sun to find the lake had surged forward over the sand, trapping them in the cave. The dogs had almost drowned.

Lucky swallowed his fears. *We have time before the lake comes back . . . for now, we should be safe.*

Sweet was the first to reach the bank. She led the Pack beneath the sleet and the howling wind, along the edges of the town. Looking out over the torn streets and damaged buildings, Lucky was relieved to see that the longpaws hadn't returned. He hoped they never would. *This place isn't safe for dogs* or *longpaws.*

They hurried as best they could along the edges of the town. Wet sand stuck to their coats and wedged itself between their claws. Lucky was careful to pause and sniff the air at regular intervals. There was no sign of the Fierce Dogs.

Sweet barked for Bella, who hurried to walk alongside them. Lucky, Sweet, and Bella fell into step, out of earshot of the other dogs.

The swift-dog shook her wet fur. "Where is the place you spoke about?"

"It's farther up the bank," Bella told her.

"But everything looks different now," Sweet pointed out. "I can see how far the lake reached over the land in the Growl. It pulled up rocks, threw down trees. . . . If the Lake-Dog broke her banks, the same is probably true of the River-Dog. How can you be so sure you'll recognize the place upstream when you reach it?"

Bella glanced at Lucky. "Remember where we saw that huge prey-creature, the one with the hard, round paws and long, flicky tail?"

Lucky remembered. For an instant, the animal's rich, peppery scent returned to him, and he licked his chops.

"It was beyond that point. I'll know when we get there." Bella's eyes traced over the sand. "The land was rugged but greener, beyond the Endless Lake, and there wasn't any sand." She gave her fur a shake and continued along the wet bank.

Looking back, Lucky could see the Pack was flagging. Sleet still fell in icy sheets, and the dogs skidded and clawed along the difficult terrain. Moon was working hard to nudge her half-grown pups forward, but it was difficult for them. Martha and Bruno were taking turns carrying Sunshine over the sodden path.

Lucky hoped it wouldn't take much longer to find Bella's spot. *What if Sweet's right about the Growl changing the landscape along the river? There might not be anywhere we could ambush the Fierce Dogs. And what if Twitch's Pack has left the forest?* He wasn't sure how long the dogs could keep going after such a stressful day. He turned back to Bella and Sweet, who were charging ahead, then looked at the swirling waters of the lake. As he climbed over a hump in the bank, the water seemed to change color, growing greener. The dogs turned a sharp bend and skirted around some rocks, and it grew less lively.

Mickey trotted up alongside Lucky. "Look! The far bank has appeared."

Lucky barked his agreement. It felt reassuring to see the bank beneath the lashing sleet. Had it been there all along? Where did it retreat to when the Lake-Dog took over from the River-Dog?

"We're almost there," said Bella, her tail wagging despite the sleet. She paused, running her snout along the wet ground.

Sweet flashed her a wary look. *She doesn't really trust Bella's judgment,* thought Lucky.

But sure enough, at the next bend in the river path, the earth became softer and more like a normal bank. Narrow blades of grass shot up from wet soil. *That's where we saw the giant prey-creature,* thought Lucky. It looked reassuringly familiar, and he felt his pent-up tension drain from his body. *Bella* does *know where she's going!* he thought proudly.

Some low trees had fallen and the earth had split, revealing its churned-up brown insides. Lucky cringed, remembering his dream where the Earth-Dog had died. He pushed it away.

"Not much farther!" barked Bella.

The river path bent again, and an outcrop of rocks towered over the path. "Here!" she barked triumphantly.

Lucky frowned. It looked different from how he'd remembered it. Rocks must have been turned on their sides and rolled by the Growl. In the darkening light, beneath heavy sleet, they were tall and menacing like jagged teeth.

Sweet's eyes roved over the rocks appreciatively as the rest of the Pack gathered around. "This is a good ambush spot," she conceded. "The rocks seem to go on for a while, and the path is narrow, so there'll be no escape but into the river. I'd love to see Blade try to make a swim for it, though we'll need to find a way to climb onto the top of the rocks."

Caught up in her Alpha's enthusiasm, Daisy climbed some low rocks and tried to scramble onto the higher slabs. There was a creaking sound from the outcrop and she tumbled backward, sending a spray of pebbles down behind her.

The other dogs cringed away from the pebbles, and Bruno almost lost his footing and slipped down the bank.

"Careful!" barked Snap.

The old dog heaved himself back onto the path with a grunt.

Daisy nibbled the ruffled fur of her flank. "I'm sorry," she murmured.

Sweet glared at her. "You need to think before you act! That's obviously not the way to do it—the rocks are sharp and high. We will have to approach them from the back." Her eyes trailed over the river path. "This way."

Lucky fell into step alongside the swift-dog as she padded along the bank. The sleet was letting up, the clouds rising and parting overhead. The air grew colder as the Sun-Dog ran for cover in his warm bed beyond the edges of the sky.

"It will be hard to see soon," Lucky whispered. "And the dogs need rest."

"I know," Sweet murmured. "Just a little farther."

They were nearly at the part of the river where the rescue party had left Twitch and his new Pack. The smell was familiar—less salty, more earthy—but it looked quite different after the Growl. A couple of the thickets of low bushes had toppled on their sides, and one bush was floating in the river, tapping the bank as though it wanted to crawl out. Between the bushes that were still standing, there seemed to be a path that wound around the back of the rocks.

Sweet turned to the Pack. "There's more vegetation on this bit of the bank. Stay here and make a camp in the undergrowth. Lucky and I will try to find a way onto the rocks."

Several of the dogs sighed with relief. Dart sank onto her hindquarters, and Martha set Sunshine down. Lucky noticed that the big black dog looked weary, and he felt a pang of sadness. She was usually so full of determination, regardless of the hardships. *The Growl has really taken its toll on all the dogs.*

Moon and Bella started sniffing out places to rest for the night. Lucky would have liked to rest too, but Sweet was already squeezing through the bushes and leaping over a fallen tree. He hurried after her. The ground was rugged and uneven, and he almost tripped on a knotted root. When he straightened up, he could see that Sweet had stopped not far ahead.

"This way," she urged.

The shrubs and earth disappeared, giving way to shafts of rock that rose steadily upward. Lucky climbed blindly, hardly able to see more than a dog-length ahead. Then the rocks parted, and he realized he and Sweet were high on the outcrop. The Moon-Dog had risen overhead. Her faint reflection skated over the river.

Lucky looked down. The path was far below them. With a shiver, he imagined the Fierce Dogs streaming along it. While the Wild Pack would have the element of surprise, and the advantage of height, it would be hard to leap down the rocks without injury. A wrong move could send them all into the river.

He turned anxiously to Sweet. "What if the plan goes wrong? It seems so risky."

Sweet gazed down at the river. "I know, Beta. I wish I had a better plan. But we have to do something, or we'll be running from Blade for the rest of our lives."

Lucky thought of his dream where the Fierce Dogs had

vanquished the Earth-Dog and were ruling the world with brutality. He edged closer to Sweet and rested his head on her shoulder.

She licked his ear. "Even if we fail, we will have given it our best . . . and at least I'll have you by my side."

CHAPTER FIFTEEN

The Sun-Dog was crouching behind a thick gray cloud, but his faint light glowed on the river. There was a hoot of a sleepy night bird, and something rustled in the frosty grass. Lucky watched, bleary-eyed, as Sweet rolled onto her paws. He was reluctant to leave the warmth of the hedgerow and the Pack, but already Sweet was stretching and other dogs were yawning noisily, rising and shaking their fur.

Soon Beetle and Thorn were gamboling about, full of energy, pouncing on each other with high-pitched growls and bounding toward the river.

"Careful, you two!" Moon called after them. "Not too near the edge, it could be slippery."

Lucky snorted white mist from his snout. Frost clung to the part of his back that had been exposed to the sky. He twisted around to lick it, feeling the chill on his tongue.

Sweet barked sharply for the Pack's attention. "Snap, lead a hunting party. Take . . ." She paused, clearly considering which dogs were best to use. With all the danger closing in on the Pack, Lucky knew that rules and roles weren't exactly Sweet's main concerns.

"Mickey and Bella," she barked finally. "I know it's tough in the Ice Wind, but there are prey-creatures around. I can smell them. Try to find something quickly. Once we have eaten, we can move on. Watch out for broken trees or other hazards since the Growl."

"Yes, Alpha," Snap replied, her small body erect. She trotted down to the riverbank with her tail high. Mickey and Bella followed, and they soon disappeared from view.

There was a light drumming of paws and Beetle returned, breathless, his litter-sister right behind him. "We've found something!" Beetle barked.

"It's really strange," added Thorn.

Sweet and Lucky followed the half-grown pups down to the riverbank.

"Look!" yipped Thorn. A thin layer of ice had formed along the surface.

Beetle turned to Lucky. "Why has the water stopped moving? Is the River-Dog okay?"

"Sometimes, when it gets really cold and the Sun-Dog is far away, water turns sharp and hard. It's frozen," Lucky told them.

"And it never moves again?" asked Thorn.

Lucky nudged her gently with his snout. "Of course it will. Perhaps later today, but perhaps not until Tree Flower, when the air becomes warmer."

Beetle shuffled closer to Thorn, shoving his litter-sister out of the way. "Will the Endless Lake freeze too?"

"I don't think so," said Lucky slowly. It was hard to imagine. *But maybe anything is possible,* he told himself, distracted for a moment by the memory of Alfie from his dream. That dog had appeared on ice . . . had that been the frozen River-Dog? Lucky looked about him anxiously. *Is this place important?* he wondered, recalling the dead dog's words. *Is it here that I'll "know what to do"? The place I will do my "duty"?* A crow cawed nearby, and his ears pricked up nervously.

Martha joined them on the riverbank. Gingerly she lowered a paw onto the ice and gave it a tap. She recoiled with a small whine.

Beetle watched her, wide-eyed. "Is River-Dog okay?" he

persisted. "You know about her, don't you? Is the cold hurting her?"

"She's just sleeping," Martha soothed, but her whiskers flexed uneasily as she watched the frozen river.

"Keep away from there!" barked Moon. "Get over here right now."

Her pups turned and hurried to her.

"We were careful," yipped Thorn.

"Careful or not, I told you it's slippery. That ice is thin, and the River-Dog is sleeping underneath it. Can you imagine how angry she'd be if you fell through the ice and woke her up?"

She led the pups back to the temporary camp among the hedges, leaving Sweet, Lucky, and Martha alone.

Lucky could see that Martha was still worried. "River-Dog will be fine," he reassured her. "When I lived in the city, the ponds in the park would sometimes freeze over during Ice Wind, but they would always spring back to life in Tree Flower."

The black dog turned her brown eyes on him. "I know, it's only . . . I can't help feeling sad. As though she died and will never come back." She drew her gaze away and shook her thick fur coat. "I'm just being silly. Tired, I expect."

Before Lucky could say any more, Martha turned and padded

along the riverbank. She sank down onto her belly and licked her paws as she stared over the frozen water.

"I should go to her," he murmured.

"Not now," replied Sweet. She craned her neck and her ears pricked up. The hunters had returned, Bella holding a pigeon in her jaws and Mickey and Snap each with rabbits. The dogs gathered around them next to the thicket.

Lucky wagged his tail approvingly. He knew it was tough to find food in this environment. This wasn't exactly a feast, but it would give every dog in the Pack a much-needed boost.

The dogs watched hungrily as Sweet tore off a succulent hunk of rabbit and fell back, indicating that it was Lucky's turn to eat. He knew that the Alpha and Beta, above all the other dogs, had to keep their strength up to protect the Pack. Still, they were careful to leave some good pieces for the weaker dogs. Not like the wolf-dog, who had eaten heartily, indifferent to his Packmates at the bottom of the ranks. There had been days when Whine and Sunshine hadn't eaten at all. Lucky glanced at the dirty white dog. A brightness had returned to her eyes.

No dog will go hungry in Sweet's Pack.

He thought of the half wolf. Would he be treated badly as Blade's Omega? He had looked skinny, the outlines of his ribs just visible beneath his fur. But Lucky could feel no sympathy for the Wild Pack's old leader. *He made his decision when he sided with the Fierce Dogs.*

As Sunshine gulped down the last of the pigeon, the dogs set out again along the river path. The Sun-Dog had pierced through the clouds, and a low light dazzled the frozen water. Soon Sweet led the Pack farther from the Endless Sea, forging a difficult path over churned-up earth and fallen hedges. They foraged deeper into the sloping valley, sniffing for signs of other dogs.

Lucky's whiskers bristled, and he looked about. The landscape was beginning to look familiar. The number of trees was steadily increasing and the earth was richer. Lucky shrank away from the occasional fallen trunk, with roots exposed and flailing in the breeze. The forest was a dangerous place to be during a Growl. His fur prickled. What if Twitch's Pack hadn't made it?

As Lucky paused, sniffing, Bella caught up with him. "Do you recognize this place?"

"I think so," he murmured. He caught the faintest whiff of Twitch's scent on the cool air. "I think this is where I first saw Terror, the mad dog."

Sweet had stopped up ahead. She turned to address the Pack. "It's cold, and we need to cover as much range as we can and get back to the rocks along the riverbank before the Sun-Dog goes to sleep. We'll move faster if we break up. I will lead one group and Lucky will take charge of another. Moon, I want you to take a third group. I will explore the flank of the valley that loops around the cliffs. Moon, double back through the forest toward the city, but don't go too far. Lucky, you head straight on, into the center of the forest."

Moon and Lucky barked their agreement.

"Be sure to call out for Twitch every few pawsteps," Sweet went on. "We don't want him to be caught unawares and think we're trying to sneak into his territory."

Daisy, Storm, and Snap were in Lucky's group. They watched as the other dogs peeled off on either side of the tree line. Then Lucky gave a small bark and led the way straight through the trees, deeper into the forest in the opposite direction from the riverbank. They advanced slowly as the trees pressed closer together. Lucky barked for Twitch every few steps, climbing over the rotting undergrowth and watching for falling branches.

Large crows cawed in the high branches, and fallen leaves crunched beneath their paws. The forest of Ice Wind was very different from the golden forest of Red Leaf. The Sun-Dog's light cut strange patterns through the bare branches, throwing twisted shadows over the uneven ground. Lucky felt edgy, keen for the Pack to be reunited.

A deep, furious roar rose over the forest, and the ground seemed to quiver. Crows took flight in panic and the dogs turned to one another, wide eyed.

"What was that?" hissed Daisy.

A moment later they heard the howl of a dog in pain.

"This way!" barked Lucky. He and the other dogs crashed through the forest, zigzagging between trees and leaping over fallen branches. They burst onto a terrifying scene.

A giantfur was rearing onto her hind legs. Her brown coat trembled with fury, and she threw back her head in a powerful roar. Drool fell from her jagged teeth as she flailed her forepaws ferociously. Her head skimmed the branches of a nearby tree, and her body was easily as thick as its trunk.

Lucky gasped, his hairs rising on end.

Cowering beneath the giantfur was a skinny, gray-furred dog. His tail was trapped under a fallen tree, and he tugged and scrabbled to free himself. His eyes fell on Lucky and the others, and he howled in desperation.

"Help me! I can't move! I've been trapped here since the Growl. Please help! I've been calling to my Pack, but the only one who has answered is the giantfur!"

The beast gave an angry snort. Thumping her paws on the ground, she moved closer to the terrified dog.

Lucky's heart raced. He didn't know how they could defeat this beast, but they couldn't leave the dog to be killed. Lucky ran to the gray dog's side, barking furiously at the giantfur, who fell silent a moment and blinked at the dogs in confusion.

Snap took her cue from Lucky, charging toward the giantfur with a volley of barks. The beast seemed to return to her senses. She swiped at Lucky with a huge paw, but Lucky ducked and sprang out of the way as the giantfur's claws skimmed his fur.

"Leave him alone, you monster!" barked Storm, rushing to Lucky's side.

The giantfur's shaggy head quivered with rage, twisting sideways as she released a deafening growl.

Daisy was barking, trying to be heard above the din. "Not like that! Don't you remember the giantfur near the white ridge, when our old Alpha sent me out with the three pups?"

Snap and Storm turned to look at her, but Lucky couldn't tear his gaze away from the beast. The giantfur's massive head had swung around, her eyes small and red-rimmed. Spit gathered at her mouth, and her muzzle crinkled with fury as she focused her attention on Daisy.

"Storm, remember?" Daisy appealed. "You were very young. Fang barked at the giantfur, and it only made things worse!"

All at once Lucky recalled the encounter on the rocks, which he and the dog-wolf had watched at a distance. Daisy was right! They needed to appease the giantfur, not anger her.

The beast was dragging a forepaw over the ground, leaving long ridges where her claws cut through the earth. She shifted her red-rimmed eyes back to Lucky, Storm, and the trapped dog, releasing another dreadful roar.

"Keep perfectly still," Daisy urged. "Lower your hackles and look away. She thinks you're challenging her."

Lucky did what he was told, stooping to the ground and dropping his gaze. Snap and Storm copied his movements. Lucky threw a quick look at the trapped dog. He still watched, wild-eyed, but he no longer barked.

"That's it," Daisy encouraged. "Now you don't seem threatening. Lucky and Snap, can you dig that dog out? Quickly . . ."

Disturbed by Daisy's yelps, the giantfur paused to watch her while Lucky and Snap fell back, furiously digging to free the trapped dog. He gave a whine of gratitude as he wiggled his tail out from under the fallen tree.

"Now back away," Daisy told them. "Slowly."

The giantfur was no longer growling as the dogs shrank back toward Daisy. As Lucky retreated, he kept his eyes on the beast. She had rolled onto her rear paws again, hovering over the dogs with menace. Her lip shook, bubbling with spit. Lucky cringed, forcing himself not to run. He cowered with the other dogs behind a tree trunk, his eyes still trained on the giantfur.

After a moment, she fell onto her forepaws with a thump, turning away from the dogs, as though she had forgotten them. She took a swipe at the fallen tree trunk, rolling it out of the way. With angry grunts she pushed and shoved between broken branches and debris.

"What's she doing?" Storm whispered.

Lucky's voice was low. "I think she wants to get inside that cave."

Sure enough, the giantfur shouldered her way into a hollow behind the fallen tree, vanishing into the darkness with a huff.

Lucky led the dogs a safe distance from the cave. The gray dog moved gingerly, pausing a few times to lick his tail. When they were at a safe distance, Lucky stopped to rest beneath a tall tree with a thick trunk, and the other dogs gathered around him. The tree was not bare like the others, though instead of leaves it had countless pointed green spikes.

Snap started cleaning her wiry coat. "Of course," she said thoughtfully. "Giantfurs sleep through Ice Wind. I remember that now, they hate the cold. The Growl must have woken her, and then that tree fell in front of her den. Which means you were in the way too," she said to the gray dog.

The dog shuddered. "I don't think my barking helped. I was calling my Pack, and it must have annoyed the giantfur. I'm glad to hear it wasn't personal, though," he murmured wryly. He straightened up and looked at Lucky and the other dogs. "You saved my life. I don't know how to thank you."

Lucky took a proper look at the gray-furred dog. He was skinny, but his lean legs flexed with muscles. "Are you a member of Twitch's Pack?"

"Yes. I'm Whisper. Do you know our Alpha?"

"He used to be in our Pack," Snap replied. "This is our Beta, Lucky, and this is Daisy and Storm."

Whisper gazed at Storm in awe. "Are you *the* Storm? The one who killed Terror?"

Lucky was instantly on edge, remembering Storm's violence that night.

Storm cocked her head. "I was at the fight, and I helped to

bring him down. I'm sorry about that. I know he was your Alpha, but he was a mean dog." She glanced uncertainly at Lucky.

He started to rise to his paws, wondering if he would have to defend her. *What if this dog was more loyal to Terror than Twitch had been?*

Lucky was surprised when Whisper threw himself at Storm's forepaws, down on his belly, then rolled onto his back with his legs in the air.

"Our new Alpha told us what you did. You liberated us from Terror! You saved our Pack! We are forever in your debt."

Storm stared at him in surprise. "I was just trying to help my friends," she murmured.

Whisper rolled onto his paws but kept his head dipped respectfully. "Then you are as loyal, brave, and humble as Twitch said."

Storm's narrow tail wagged at this, and she panted cheerfully. Lucky felt happy too. *Maybe she was wrong to kill Terror the way she did, but Storm is loyal, and it's about time she received some praise.*

He glanced out into the surrounding trees. "Where is the rest of your Pack?"

"I don't know. Everyone scattered when the Growl hit, and no dog has heard my cries for help, so they must not be near."

"Is your tail okay?" asked Daisy, giving it a sniff. It seemed to have a strange bend near the beginning.

Whisper looked over his shoulder. "I think it may be broken, but it doesn't hurt too much, and the main thing is that I'm alive. I didn't expect to be when I saw the giantfur."

At that moment Sweet's howl rose over the forest, calling for Twitch. A second later, the dogs heard a bark in reply.

"It sounds like she's found your Pack," yapped Snap, her tail lashing.

Whisper gave a quick wag of his tail and flinched. "Ouch. I'm very happy, but I need to remember not to do that for a while," he said with a good-natured tilt of the head.

Lucky barked to Sweet and Twitch, leading the rest of his group through the woods until he saw the swift-dog's slender frame appear between the trees. Moon and her group were already there, greeting each of Twitch's Pack in turn. Lucky made a quick count of the dogs: There was Twitch himself and his black Beta, Splash, Whisper, and five other dogs Lucky didn't know.

The floppy-eared Alpha yipped and wagged his tail, exchanging friendly licks with his old Pack. "Lucky! You're here!" He bounded forward with great agility, despite having only three legs. His Pack approached respectfully, pleased to see Whisper among the Wild Dogs. Lucky greeted Twitch, then hurried to Sweet's side, breathing in her warm scent. Even though they had only been parted for a short time, he found that he had missed her.

"I didn't expect to see you in the woods," said Twitch. "I hope you plan to stay a while. You are all welcome." His eyes trailed over the Wild Pack. "But wait . . . where is Spring?" He turned to Lucky and Sweet with an inquisitive look. "Where is my littermate?"

CHAPTER SIXTEEN

The Sun-Dog's light flickered between branches as Lucky, Sweet, and Twitch climbed onto the huge, smooth trunk of a fallen tree. There was a faint hum of insects and the rustling sound of wind over broken twigs. The twigs shimmered white with frost. The two Packs were gathered a rabbit-chase away, sharing some kill that Twitch's hunters had buried before the Growl. *That was clever of them,* thought Lucky. *We should learn from that—store more food and think ahead.*

Sweet turned from the Packs to Twitch, who was looking pensive. "It is good of you to share your food."

Twitch flicked his floppy ears. "Of course. You are always welcome. And Daisy's quick thinking saved Whisper. It's lucky you came along when you did."

Sweet's voice dropped to a gentle whimper. "I'm sorry we

came with bad news about your litter-sister."

Twitch dipped his head in acknowledgment and fell silent for a while. Yips rose from the two Packs as they finished their meal and played between the trees.

"I didn't know Spring very well," Lucky admitted. "But she was always a good, loyal dog who put the Pack first. She never shirked her responsibilities and was quick to help and defend the others. She was brave until the end."

Twitch gave a long whine. "I was sorry that a distance had formed between us since I left your Pack. I don't think she really forgave me. I'm glad that she was happy there." His whiskers flexed as he looked out across the forest toward the other dogs. "But I had my own Pack to think about. I didn't expect that, but I wasn't going to abandon them. And it wasn't as though I could return to the half wolf's Pack. He took me for a deserter—he would never have let me come back." Twitch shook his coat, looking about. He turned to Sweet with his head cocked. "What happened to him? Did he die too?"

"He's alive," she said icily. "He disappeared when we fought the Fierce Dogs. But then we discovered that he's joined Blade's Pack . . . as her *Omega*."

Twitch stared at the swift-dog in disbelief.

"He thinks he's on the winning side," she explained. Lucky could tell she was trying to sound matter-of-fact, but he heard the anger in Sweet's voice. "And Blade has all sorts of strange ideas about the end of the world."

Lucky watched as Twitch frowned, his ears raised slightly. It was odd to see their former Packmate—the Patrol Dog too injured to be taken seriously by the half wolf—talking to Sweet, his former Beta, as an equal. *In the wolf-dog's rigid structure, dogs were too quickly dismissed. That will no longer happen in Sweet's Pack.*

Lucky lowered his head respectfully. He felt a sort of wonder that two Pack leaders could meet like this, without a fight. The half dog would never have talked this way. Anger fizzed at the back of Lucky's throat. *That traitor . . .* Their old Alpha had been wrong in dismissing Twitch. *He was wrong about a lot of things.*

Sweet filled Twitch in about Blade's prophecies, Fang's brutal death, and the plan to kill Storm. She finished with her realization that they must confront the Fierce Dogs and Whine's decision to leave the Pack.

Twitch cocked his head. "You're going to fight Blade?"

"We know it won't be easy," Sweet replied. "But we have to put an end to all this." She watched him evenly. "That's where you come in."

Lucky watched Twitch, whose eyes were fixed on Sweet. What happened now could change the fortunes of their Pack. Lucky's muscles twitched beneath his coat, and he licked his lips nervously.

Sweet continued, "If our Packs join forces, we would have a real chance of overthrowing the Fierce Dogs. We may not be as strong as them, but together we would outnumber them. We have some great fighters, and we'd have the advantage of surprise."

Lucky held his breath. If Twitch refused them now, they wouldn't have the numbers to fight Blade. He shuddered. *How long will the Pack keep defending Storm when the Fierce Dogs appear?*

"I'm sorry, Sweet," said Twitch, his voice quiet but resolute. "I want to help you, but I am the Alpha of this Pack. It isn't a position I'd ever anticipated, and it isn't one I chose for myself. But as their Alpha, I won't bring my Pack into danger lightly. They suffered a lot under Terror. Since his death, we've had a peaceful time where the dogs have been able to recover. Some are still nervous, damaged by Terror's brutality. It wouldn't be right to ask them to fight—and it isn't our fight to have."

Lucky's heart sank. "Couldn't you ask them to choose? Those who want to fight to protect Storm can—the others who aren't up to fighting could stay behind in the forest."

Twitch gave Lucky a sideways look. "You obviously don't know my Pack very well."

"What do you mean?"

Twitch hopped off the trunk and made his way between the trees. "Come and see."

Lucky and Sweet jumped after him, and the three dogs returned to their Packs. While the Wild Pack turned lazily to see their Alpha and Beta, looking untroubled, Twitch's Pack sprang to attention, their bodies lowered and heads dipped submissively. The dogs surrounded Twitch, awaiting instruction.

He lifted his muzzle. "Lie down on your backs and show your bellies!"

To Lucky's amazement, all seven dogs fell to the ground and rolled onto their backs, exposing their bellies. The Wild Pack watched them, exchanging surprised looks.

"Back onto your paws," Twitch ordered, and his Pack immediately complied. He turned to Sweet. "My dogs aren't used to thinking for themselves."

Lucky ran his tongue over his nose. A memory of Terror returned to him—the crazy Alpha had abused his Pack, forcing them to cower before him. Those bullied, terrified dogs had hardly dared to breathe without his command. Twitch was right—they weren't used to questioning authority.

Twitch blinked apologetically at Sweet. "If it was just me, I would join you, but I have to think of my Pack now. If I ask them to fight, they *will* fight—to the death. I don't think it's the right thing to do. It isn't fair on them."

Lucky couldn't keep the whine from his voice. "But you heard what Sweet told you. Blade has sworn not to stop until Storm is dead."

Storm thumped a tan paw on the ground. "No, Twitch is right. It isn't their fight, Lucky. I don't expect any dogs to risk their lives for me."

"I'm sorry," said Twitch. "If I could help, I would. But my Pack has already suffered enough."

All at once, several dogs began speaking, as Lucky tried to tell Storm that they would still defeat Blade, and Twitch insisted that they couldn't help.

A small but determined voice rose over the yelps. "Alpha . . . what if we *want* to fight?"

The other dogs fell silent as Whisper padded nervously toward Twitch. "I know your decision is final, and you are wise and must

SURVIVORS: STORM OF DOGS

be obeyed. But I just thought, well, Storm saved us from Terror. And again, today, she helped to rescue me from the giantfur." He risked a glance at the young Fierce Dog. "She is courageous and good. If she is in danger, I *want* to fight to protect her."

Hope swelled in Lucky's chest. He was about to turn to Twitch to see what the Pack leader thought when he heard the crunching of foliage and a small wiry-furred black dog stepped forward, stopping at Whisper's side. Lucky recognized him as Splash.

"What is it, Beta?" Twitch asked.

Splash lowered his head. "I would fight for her too, if you allow it, Alpha. Terror ruined our lives. It is thanks to this young Fierce Dog that we are free from him."

There was a murmur of agreement from the forest dogs. A small ginger-furred dog yapped and wagged her tail furiously, her eyes bright. "We'll do as our Alpha orders, but I agree with Splash. I want to help Storm."

"Thank you for speaking up, Chase." Twitch glanced at Sweet and Lucky before turning to address them. "It seems to me that some of you are keen to show your gratitude to Storm. Rake, Woody, Breeze? Omega? What do you say?"

As he spoke, the four remaining dogs of his Pack stepped

forward one after the other and stood to attention.

"We'll go where you lead, Alpha," said one, a scrawny male with wiry fur and a network of long white scars across his muzzle. "But we're ready to fight. We can never repay what Storm and these other dogs did for us." The stocky brown male beside him nodded.

"Yes," said the small black female Omega, in a voice no louder than a mouse's squeak.

"It would be an honor to fight beside the dogs who defeated Terror," said the last dog, a small brown female with large ears and short fur, meeting Lucky's eyes for a long moment before bowing her head respectfully.

"Thank you, Breeze. Very well. I would not have asked you to fight for another Pack, but if you fight willingly, we can join them." He glanced at Sweet and Lucky, who wagged their tails gratefully. Then he turned back to address his Pack, raising his voice, his head high and his bark commanding. "We will not leave our friends to battle the Fierce Dogs alone. We will fight alongside Sweet's Pack, to protect Storm and for the good of all dogs."

His Pack howled their agreement, and Storm turned to

Martha with glittering eyes. The black dog licked her on the nose and murmured something that Lucky couldn't hear. He sighed with deep relief as the two Packs pranced and yapped excitedly. Sunshine spun in tight circles, and Daisy bounded up to Whisper and nudged his muzzle with her own, her short tail thrashing.

As the Sun-Dog started sinking between the trees, the Packs squeezed through the thickets of tangled hedges to the base of the rocky outcrop. It was here, hidden behind the rocks, that they would wait to ambush the Fierce Dogs. Snap and Moon clambered over the hardstone, looking for the best points from which to launch an attack and discussing strategy with Twitch's dogs.

Sweet, Lucky, and Bella joined Twitch and Splash beneath a moss-covered tree to talk through the next move.

"Someone has to go and challenge Blade to a one-on-one fight with Storm," said Sweet.

"It needs to be a member of our Pack," Bella pointed out. "Blade can't know that we've teamed up with Twitch."

"Are you sure she'll come?" Twitch asked.

Lucky's voice was somber. "Blade will come. She's desperate to get her paws on Storm."

Overhearing her name, Storm approached. "Do you think I should go? Won't it look strange if some other dog challenges Blade for me?"

"No!" barked Lucky, Sweet, and Twitch in unison.

Sweet was emphatic. "Even if we all went to the Fierce Dogs together, you wouldn't be able to come. Blade might decide to attack you there, and it would spoil our plan. We have to lure her out to the rocks, where her Pack will be more vulnerable."

Storm nodded, though she still looked ready to argue the point.

Lucky spoke quickly. "I could take the message. I've been to Blade's camp before, and I don't think Blade would kill me on sight. She's too desperate to reach Storm."

Twitch didn't look so sure. "What if you're wrong? If, like you say, the Fierce Dogs won't play fair, they might reject the challenge and just attack you. They know that you will always stand between Storm and them, so they might use the opportunity to take you out."

"I couldn't take on Blade's Pack, but I can outrun them." Lucky ran his tongue over his lips. "I'll be on the lookout for an attack. If anything happens, I'll run as fast as I can and lead the

Fierce Dogs here." Lucky wondered at his own determination to confront Blade. *Is this the "duty" that Alfie spoke of in my dream?*

Sweet's muzzle was tense. "I don't like it. I don't like to think of Lucky approaching the Fierce Dogs' lair alone. But I believe in my Beta's ability to get himself out of almost any situation. I know he is the best dog for the job."

Lucky blinked at her affectionately. *The worst thing about all this will be leaving Sweet, even for one night.* He couldn't let himself think it might be more than a night—that he might never come back.

He peered into the naked branches of the trees. The crows were back, filling the forest with their eerie caws. The Sun-Dog's tail was pink and gold as it swept between the branches. Soon it would be dark.

Lucky rose to his paws. "I should go now. I can sleep somewhere en route. That way I can reach the Fierce Dogs' camp by sunup tomorrow, when they'll be sleepy and less likely to be in fighting spirits."

"They're *always* in fighting spirits," Storm said gloomily.

"And at sunup they'll be well rested and will be angry to be woken up," added Bella, her head cocked in concern. "Maybe I should come with you."

Lucky turned to her. He would have loved to have the company, but he knew it wasn't a good idea. "They'll be suspicious if there are two of us, and it'll be harder to encourage Blade to come without her Pack. I know she probably won't anyway, but challenging her to a battle with Storm is the best way to lure her out of her lair. With two of us, she'd be scared we might attack her." He shook his head, thinking of Alfie again. "I have to do this alone."

He said his good-byes to the Pack, giving Sweet a lick on the nose.

"Be careful," she murmured, as she had the last time they'd parted on the cliffs at the edge of their camp.

"I'll see you again very soon," Lucky assured her. He gave a quick wag of his tail, but beneath his confident demeanor, doubt gnawed at his belly. Even if he was careful—if he stayed far enough from the Fierce Dogs' lair to run if he had to—there was always a chance they could trap him again. Lucky tried not to think about it as he wove through the tangled forest and retraced his steps on the river path.

Instead he went over their plan. He had seen the fervor in Blade's eyes—he knew she was desperate to kill Storm. *She'll follow me,* he told himself. *Her deputies will have already explored our camp— she'll know that we've left. She won't want to miss an opportunity to find the last living Fierce Dog pup born after the Big Growl.* These thoughts gave him some comfort, and he picked up his pace. But a quiet dread gathered in his belly as he advanced along the edge of the frozen river. The Fierce Dogs were so powerful and organized.

Even with the help of Twitch's Pack, did the Wild Dogs really have the strength to defeat them?

CHAPTER SEVENTEEN

A final blaze of red fur sparkled on the frozen river as the Sun-Dog ducked out of sight. Lucky wondered where the Spirit Dog slept in the land beyond the horizon. Was it always safe and warm there? Did the Forest-Dog and River-Dog ever visit him?

The wind rose above the river, but even its angry breath couldn't budge the ice. Lucky's tail clung to his flank as night settled over the forest. He could no longer see the trees beyond the long rocky outcrop, but he knew they were there. He stood still, straining his ears. The dark forest was so quiet during Ice Wind. In Tree Flower, there was always the chirp of birds, even at night. There was the rustling of leaves and the thrum of insects. Ice Wind was a quieter time.

A lonelier time.

At least the Moon-Dog had appeared. She seemed to be

leading him as she slunk out from behind a bank of cloud. The air was clear but achingly cold. *I should find somewhere to sleep—if I have to run from the Fierce Dogs, I'll need my strength.* As the rocky outcrop came to an end, he sniffed about for a makeshift den, but something gave him pause. *Is it safe to stop moving?*

The night was so bitterly cold he could see his breath rising in tiny clouds as he panted. The air tasted strange. Lucky put out his tongue and then quickly drew it back, realizing that he had felt this odd texture in the air before.

Snow is coming.

He'd seen snow once or twice before, back when he was living in the city. It had lit up the trees and buildings with its fair pelt. It had never been a danger to him. But then he thought of Ferret Tooth, the Lone Dog who had begged for scraps outside the Food House—the dog who had curled up in the park one cold Ice Wind night and had never gotten up again. Lucky kept walking.

I was a Lone Dog once, just like Ferret Tooth.

It was strange to think of those times now. Lucky could remember the city before the Big Growl only in vague terms. The Food House, the Mall, and the houses where the longpaws lived. He had enjoyed his independence back then and had never felt like he needed a Pack. *I didn't have to worry about other dogs,* he reminded himself. His paw skidded on some icy pebbles, and he caught his balance. *I was totally free. I could get up when I wanted, eat when I wanted. . . .*

As these thoughts circled Lucky's mind, he wondered for the first time if they were really true. *The Food House was only worth visiting when the longpaws were around. Some of them shooed me away, but friendlier ones would offer me scraps. And it was always best to search the spoil-boxes at the end of the day, after the longpaws had filled them.*

Lucky's tail drooped as it struck him that he had never really supported himself—he had always relied on the longpaws. *I thought I was free of the longpaws, but it was their food that kept me fed, their tall houses that sheltered me from the wind. I never even hunted, not back then.* Pausing, Lucky frowned, tracing the hard earth with a forepaw. *Was I really any different from a Leashed Dog? I needed the longpaws every bit as much as Mickey or Sunshine. Maybe I only thought I was better, more independent.*

His head dipped with shame at this realization. *How foolish I must have seemed to Sweet back then, refusing to leave the city. It's only now, as a Pack Dog, that I'm truly free.*

The clouds had dispersed, leaving a jet-black sky with endless stars. Shivers ran along Lucky's spine. The grass blades on the bank were already sparkling with frost, and he felt it creeping up his paws. He could smell the first whiff of the Endless Lake.

Soon he would be passing the long wooden walkway over the water, with the little houses where the rescue party had hidden from the Fierce Dogs. *Fang helped us by telling Blade he hadn't seen us,* he remembered with a stab of sadness for the young dog. Poor, foolish Fang—loyal to the wrong Pack.

Lucky thought of his own Pack. Beautiful Sweet, his mate and Alpha, good-hearted Martha, loyal Mickey, and all the others. It soothed him to think of them curled up together, safe beyond the rocky outcrop. Wherever they were, that was where he wanted to be, and no makeshift shelter would ever be the same.

His legs started aching with fatigue, and his thoughts grew melancholy as he crunched over the frosty ground. *I need sleep, but I don't dare stop when it's this cold—not unless I find somewhere decent to rest.* He thought of Blade and her ferocious Pack. It was dangerous to approach them if he was tired. He needed to have his wits about him. He might have to think on his feet. And what if they gave chase? *They'll tear me to shreds!*

He pictured their pointed fangs, then reproached himself sharply, picking up the pace. It wasn't helpful to think of such things after nightfall. "Bad thoughts infect a pup's dreams," Lucky's Mother-Dog had warned him once. He tried to think of good things, like the taste of a juicy rabbit after a kill. But it was no use—his mind kept returning to the Fierce Dogs. The great battle was coming at last. He had dreamed about it so many times. When the snow came, the fighting would start—and he would be powerless to stop it.

No, he told himself. *It won't go the way of my visions. We have a plan— we have the help of Twitch's Pack.* Would the ambush work? He tried not to imagine the Fierce Dogs savaging his friends, pinning them down and mauling them. But the more he tried to squeeze out the images, the more vivid they became. He could almost smell the metallic scent of blood on the freezing air.

By the time he reached the outskirts of the longpaw town, Lucky's legs felt heavy and chilled to the bone. It was silent and deserted, the tall, broken buildings rising up at strange angles. Ordinary objects became spooky in the pale light of the Moon-Dog. Shattered clear-stone gleamed like deadly fangs. A collapsed tree looked like a hunching monster preparing to pounce.

Lucky padded warily over the torn hardstone streets. His paws slipped on patches of ice, and he slunk past debris left by the second Growl. He followed a path to the pointed railings of a park. Some had bent and fallen in a heap, and he leaped over them, landing on overgrown grass.

Lucky's mind drifted to Blade and her prophecy. *She murdered her own pup.* The thought haunted him. A Mother-Dog who was prepared to do that would think nothing of killing countless other dogs. *She is so sure of Earth-Dog's wrath. She's bound to see the latest Growl as a sign of things to come.* Despite himself, he couldn't help a wave of fear as he remembered Blade's conviction that she knew what must be done. *What if she's right about Earth-Dog seeking a sacrifice? What if her dreams about Storm are true?*

He looked up into the dark sky with a guilty pang. Storm wasn't even fully grown. She was harmless.

Harmless . . .

In an instant he saw Terror's bloodied face, his lower jaw ripped away and dropped onto the ground like a hunk of prey. Lucky remembered the frenzied yellow eyes and the horrible gurgling that had come from the mad dog's throat. And he remembered the look of triumph on Storm's face as she licked Terror's blood off her whiskers.

Lucky sighed, feeling very small beneath the twinkling stars. Would the Spirit Dogs really care about him, or Storm, or other dogs in this torn-up world?

On instinct, he threw back his head and howled. "O Spirit Dogs, what will happen to us? Is Blade right—will a final Growl come that puts an end to everything? Will there be snow and a

Storm of Dogs? How can I protect my Pack?"

What if leading the Fierce Dogs to Sweet and the other Wild Dogs goes horribly wrong? What if we're overpowered? Should we have run after all?

No reassuring image came to him from the Spirit Dogs, and Lucky whimpered, fear creeping along his spine. *Maybe they've given up on me. Blade seems to know what's going on—could they be protecting her?*

Lucky looked about, gripped with fear. There was no scent of anyone—not a rabbit, not a longpaw, not even a lone bird. The tall buildings of the town blocked the wind. It was so quiet and deserted that Lucky felt as though he was completely alone in the world.

His eyes trailed along the dark contours of the overgrown park. They rested on a tree—the first he had seen in the town that was still standing totally upright. *Even here, even after the Growl, could the Forest-Dog be near?* This thought gave him a little bit of comfort. He had a strong impulse to find shelter. *The Forest-Dog will care for me and protect me from the cold.*

The fear in Lucky's heart eased and he crossed the park, squeezing himself between broken railings and out onto the street. He padded along the hardstone until he found a longpaw house with its door hanging off at an angle. Sliding under the broken door, he crept inside.

Lucky stepped furtively through a dark corridor. The smell of longpaws was faint—they couldn't have returned here after the first Growl, not even to sniff around. He found a pile of old soft-hides and dragged them against a wall, sneezing as dust rose from them and filled the air. At least the hides were warm and the worst of the chill was kept out by the thick walls of the building. Lucky didn't like the thought that he was relying on longpaws again—hiding away in their huge dens, using their soft-hides—but it couldn't be helped. He lowered his head onto the hides with a long whine and was soon fast asleep.

Lucky opened his eyes and gazed up into the piercing sunlight. The Sun-Dog was bounding over the Endless Lake, lighting the waves so they sparkled blue like the Sky-Dogs. From his vantage point on the cliffs, he could just hear the distant sigh of the tumbling water as it lapped against the sand. He stretched his legs and yawned, rolling onto his back. The Sun-Dog tickled his belly with his warming rays. From the corner of his eye, Lucky saw a rabbit shoot out from a hole and hop between the grass stems. The prey-creature paused to wash its forepaws, and Lucky watched lazily. He didn't give chase. His belly was already full, and the Pack had plenty of kill left over from their morning hunt.

Instead Lucky batted absently at a fly that swooped above his nose. Birds twittered in the nearby trees and foraged for worms in the valley, now a meadow bursting with wildflowers and butterflies. A deep sensation of contentment ran through Lucky's fur.

He heard a series of high-pitched yaps and climbed onto his paws. Pups! Lucky trod through the long grass stems toward the circle of trees by the pond. He could see four puppies sitting on flat rocks, their heads cocked in concentration. Lucky took in their fuzzy, narrow bodies, their large soft heads, and their floppy ears. They all had slender muzzles and dark-brown eyes, but two had sandy fur, one a deeper tan coat, and the last had fur as dark as her eyes.

A short distance away was a dark, looming shape. A chill cut through Lucky's heart, and his breath caught in his throat. A Fierce Dog!

She rose on her powerful legs, the muscles rippling beneath her glossy coat. Then she noticed Lucky, acknowledging him with a wag of her tail. This was no deadly attack-dog—it was Storm, all grown up!

"What happened then?" whined the sandy pup with shaggy fur.

"Yes, Storm, what happened then?" yipped the others.

Storm's eyes widened dramatically. "Then the ground started quivering so hard that trees shook and fell to the ground! The dogs turned to one another, wondering if it was the end of the world."

"And was it?" asked the dark brown pup in a small voice. She was as slender as a swift-dog, but her fur was longer and looked fuzzy to the touch.

"Of course it wasn't," said the short-furred sandy pup. She raised her muzzle self-importantly, reminding Lucky of Bella when she was young. "Otherwise

Storm wouldn't be here to tell the story!"

"I almost wasn't," said the Fierce Dog seriously. "Everything shook, the End-less Lake went wild, the cliffs crumbled, and the sky turned dark."

"Even the Earth-Dog couldn't shake the whole world!" gasped the fourth pup, cocking her tan head in disbelief.

"But she did," said Storm. "I know—I was there! It happened just before the great battle, the Storm of Dogs."

The pups must have heard the term before, as they all gasped, blinking at one another and turning back to the Fierce Dog. "What happened then?" they whined in unison.

"The battle was terrible!" she told them, her floppy ears pricking up. "Every dog fought to the death. The Packs clashed, and all you could hear were barks and howls. Not every dog made it. . . ." Storm's voice grew softer.

"Why were the dogs fighting?" asked the little dark brown pup.

"A crazed dog called Blade forced the battle—she was sure the world would end if she didn't. She thought Earth-Dog growled because she was mad and that she'd be even angrier if she wasn't appeased. Secretly, I think Blade just wanted a good fight—and she was going to fight no matter what."

The puppies shuddered and pressed closer together.

"And your Mother-Dog and Father-Dog were very brave. We wouldn't have beat her without them."

The pups barked and turned to look at Lucky in admiration.

"Did you fight the mean dog, Father?" asked the slender dark brown pup.

"Your Father-Dog had an important role in the battle," said Storm.

"What was it?" asked the shaggy-furred pup.

"Did he kill a bad dog?" asked the short-furred sandy pup.

Storm glanced at Lucky, her eyes twinkling enigmatically. Then she turned back to the puppies. "Your Father-Dog has always had an ear to the Spirit Dogs. They spoke to him and showed him the way—and when the time came, he knew what to do."

The pups looked at Lucky. Suddenly he knew what their names were.

Forest, Sky, River, and Earth . . .

Sky, the short-furred sandy pup, burst forward with a shrill yap. "Our Father-Dog, a hero!"

The other pups ran after her. They crowded around Lucky, a yipping, squirming, licking bundle of fur. He was buried beneath their warm, sweet bodies.

When Lucky blinked away sleep, it was just getting light. He padded through the silent longpaw house. A calm had come over him. Not all dreams were filled with shadows. . . . He had imagined a future where the Pack lived in peace, without the terror of the Fierce Dogs, where Storm was happy and where Sweet had mothered a beautiful litter of pups.

Our pups.

A wave of gratitude ran through him for the Spirit Dogs, who had visited Lucky in his loneliness and brought him hope. He set off for Blade's camp with a spring in his step. He had seen a future of darkness and terror, but he had also seen one of joy and peace. The second future, where his pups were free beneath the Sun-Dog's light, would keep him going through the dark times to come. He would fight to his last breath to make that dream come true.

CHAPTER EIGHTEEN

A thin light clung over the Endless Lake as Lucky crept over the broken streets to the border of the town. Split hardstone gave way to sand, sloping down to the water's edge. Debris bobbed on the frothing waves. Lucky could make out the wheel of a loudcage, a spoil-box, and what looked like a jumble of soft-hides tossing in the current. White waterbirds swooped overhead, screeching like angry sharpclaws. At least it was a sign of life. Despite his sense of solitude, Lucky reminded himself that he wasn't alone.

With a start, he detected a familiar scent that made his blood run cold. *Fierce Dogs!* He wasn't alone *at all*.

He backed along the edge of a street and shrank against the wall as three attack-dogs marched over the high bank of the Endless Lake. They slammed down their paws with ferocious self-assurance, kicking up sand. Lucky wondered whether Blade had brought her Pack to the town, but sniffing about, he didn't think so. *It's just a patrol. They are on the lookout . . . probably keeping a special watch for Sweet's Pack—for Storm. Blade will be keen for news.*

He watched as the attack-dogs looped back along the waterfront and strutted toward the cliffs. It was just as he'd thought—they were returning to the dark lair nestled along the rocks, near the Wild Pack's camp. *They must have figured out that we've gone.* This was bound to infuriate Blade. Lucky knew that the leader of the Fierce Dogs wasn't about to let Storm out of her grasp—her Pack would soon be hunting for the young dog over each broken street, across every deserted valley. He shuddered, thinking of the Wild Pack hiding upstream.

Well, they won't have to search for long, thought Lucky. Steeling himself, he rose up on his paws. Avoiding the patrol, he cut through side streets to climb farther up the bank of the lake. He retraced the rocky path through the cliffs, careful to avoid the unstable cliff face. His paws slipped on the icy ground, and he ordered himself to slow down. If he lost his footing now, he might tumble backward and be smashed against the rocks. It wasn't just about him—the whole Pack was counting on Lucky.

By the time he approached the lair within the cave, the Sun-Dog had risen over the cliffs. The light was misty, partially concealed by twisting clouds. Lucky stalked low to the ground, hiding behind a ridge of rock a good rabbit-chase away. From this distance, there was no sign that the Fierce Dogs' lair had been damaged in the Growl. Lucky felt a twinge of disappointment. If Blade had been injured or even killed . . . but no, he would have to go through with the plan.

He took a deep breath, remembering the warmth and safety he had felt in his dream. Pausing in his stride, he allowed the memory of its peace and tranquility to wash over him. It gave him confidence as he opened his jaws and howled Blade's name.

There was an anxious twitter of birds, but no dog emerged from Blade's lair. Lucky cocked his head, ears pricked. Had he heard a bark? He howled again, throwing more force into his voice.

"Blade!"

This time Lucky was sure he'd heard barking from within the cave. There was a scuffling of paws and several Fierce Dogs burst out, with Blade in the lead. She caught sight of Lucky, who hovered by the rock wall, staring straight at her. He stood his ground, even as Blade's lips gaped open and her teeth gnashed with a furious snarl.

"City Rat! Have you forgotten your previous visit?"

Lucky thought he should have shivered at the sight of her

bared teeth, but instead he only felt the warmth of his dream tingle through his fur. *Blade is just a tyrant and a bully. She rules with fear, with no respect for loyalty or honor. Look at Fang. . . .* Lucky pushed away the memory of the bleeding dog. *Blade has had her time,* he thought angrily, *but she is destined to be defeated.* The thought gave him courage.

Blade must have seen something on Lucky's face that made her hesitate. She stopped in her tracks, her fur visibly rising along her back in dark spikes. Her deputies, Mace and Dagger, stood just behind her, with several other Fierce Dogs guarding the entrance to the cave, their dark heads dropped threateningly.

Blade glared at Lucky. "Surely even you are not stupid enough to come back here alone. Where is the rest of your pathetic Pack?"

Lucky cleared his throat. "Our Alpha is not interested in a battle with you. You spoke of Earth-Dog's fury, and you were right—a second Growl came. It broke off the edges of the cliffs and stirred Lake-Dog into a fury. Our Alpha does not want to anger the Spirit Dogs. Your fight is with Storm, not with all of our Pack. Combat between our Packs will only lead to unnecessary bloodshed."

"Your bloodshed," growled Blade contemptuously. "Not ours."

Lucky kept his voice steady. "There is no need to involve our Packs in this. Your issue is with Storm, and she has challenged

SURVIVORS: STORM OF DOGS

you to a fair fight. She will meet you by the frozen riverbank, past the longpaw town and their broken wooden ledge that sprawls over the Endless Lake. On the banks of the river, where the forest begins, Storm will meet you to fight it out. She will wait for you alone as the Sun-Dog rises tomorrow. And she will defeat you in single combat."

Blade sneered. "That pup? Defeat *me*?"

Mace and Dagger barked in amusement, and the other Fierce Dogs echoed them.

A shiver ran along Lucky's back. If Blade refused the challenge, their plan would be for nothing. He thought of Sweet's and Twitch's Packs, gathered in the cold by the rock face, waiting for him to return.

The Fierce Dog Alpha relaxed visibly. Her nerves at seeing Lucky so bold seemed to have vanished, and some of her former cool swagger returned. "I am glad that the pup has finally seen fit to offer herself up to the Earth-Dog as sacrifice. She is deeply deluded if she thinks she can beat me, but if it's a fight she wants, it's a fight she'll get." Blade's lip wrinkled scornfully. "You can tell the pup I'll be there. And she'd better be prepared to be ripped open so the rats can finish her off. I was merciful with her litter-brothers—when the time came, their deaths were fast. Storm will not be treated with the same . . . compassion."

Lucky's muzzle tensed. He remembered Fang's brutal death with a sickening twist of his belly. *Blade doesn't know the meaning of compassion.*

Her hackles rose threateningly. "Now run and tell Storm *that*, City Dog. And run fast! You have exactly two heartbeats to get out of my sight, or we'll deliver the answer to Storm ourselves, along with your pelt as a trophy."

Lucky spun on his paws and shot over the rocks, darting between hedges toward the Wild Pack's deserted camp, toward the passage that wove between the rocks and down to the Endless Lake. He knew he had to be quick. He couldn't trust Blade to stick to the rules. The Fierce Dog might guess that his Pack was hiding near the riverbank. If she gave chase now, she would find them—he needed to tell Sweet that the attack-dogs were coming.

CHAPTER NINETEEN

The clouds had drawn in by the time Lucky reached the winding river-

bank. The sky was metallic, a glistening gray, but no rain fell in the

murky air. Lucky stopped to look up between the bare branches

of a tree. An icy wisp spun down toward him, fizzing on his nose.

He recoiled with a whine, remembering the foul black snow that

had fallen in the forest, upstream by the Pack's old camp as he'd

searched for Mickey. He sniffed carefully. There was no hint of

foulness in the air. A flake landed at his paws, small and white.

He gave it a gentle tap, and it melted with a cool tingle. *Don't be silly,*

Lucky berated himself. *It's just ordinary snow.*

Still, he slowed his pace a little, advancing more cautiously

between the foliage and weaving a path behind the rocky outcrop,

watching as the snow twirled and fell on the hedges. He could

already sense his Pack. His tail wagged in anticipation, and he thought of Sweet with her soft, velvety coat and her delicious smell.

He pushed through the undergrowth and was greeted by a sight that warmed his heart. The two Packs were curled together in a tight circle, keeping each other warm. Lucky held back a moment, enjoying the scene. Whisper was licking Storm's ears, Mickey and Snap were pressed next to Splash, and Twitch was talking to Sweet in hushed tones. Lucky cocked his head, gazing through the undergrowth. He was about to announce his presence when Daisy gave a shrill yelp.

"Look at the rain. It's falling in white lumps!"

Storm sprang to her paws with a growl. "And it *feels* different. Sort of soft but colder than usual."

Beetle and Thorn started running in tight circles.

"It isn't disappearing when it reaches the ground!" Thorn whined. "Something has gone wrong with the rain!"

"Maybe the Sky-Dogs are angry!" Beetle whimpered, scrambling to his Mother-Dog's side. "Is it something to do with the Growl?"

"It's okay, young dogs," Moon soothed. "This is called snow. It isn't anything to be scared of. When the Ice Wind is deep and takes hold of the land, sometimes even the Sky-Dogs feel the chill. Their fur bristles from the cold and their rain turns soft and white."

Storm looked up accusingly. "But why now? Are you *sure* the Sky-Dogs aren't angry, like Lake-Dog was when the Growl came back?"

Martha rose and gathered Storm and Thorn toward her. "It's just snow, like Moon said. It won't hurt us."

"And when it gets warmer, the snow will melt into water, just like rain," Moon assured them. "And Earth-Dog will lap it up."

"Why doesn't she do that now?" Daisy asked. "Is it too cold for Earth-Dog?"

"Yes," Moon murmured. "Snow is very cold, and that isn't how Earth-Dog likes it. She will wait until the snow melts to rain. Then she will drink it and it will all disappear."

This seemed to reassure Daisy, and she breathed slowly through her nose, releasing a cloud of steam. She settled by Martha's side as all the dogs gazed into the snow, falling silent in its soft hush.

Lucky felt a rush of affection for his Pack. He opened his mouth, about to bark his arrival, but he caught a strange scent and froze. *A Fierce Dog!*

It wasn't Storm. Some other Fierce Dog was here. There was

only one scent, but that didn't reassure Lucky. He shrank back into the undergrowth and stalked around the edge of the little makeshift camp, treading lightly so as not to make a sound. Fear bristled along Lucky's neck, and he fought to stay calm, trying to remember the warmth and peace of his dream—if he panicked now, the Fierce Dog might smell his fear-scent.

As Lucky watched, concealed beneath behind a snowy branch, the Fierce Dog came into view. His muscles flexed beneath his short black fur and he panted heavily, wild-eyed, as though he had been running for many rabbit-chases. Lucky recognized the trespasser as Arrow, the young Fierce Dog who'd been fortunate enough to have been born just before the Big Growl. Arrow's eyes were fixed on the Packs. He didn't notice Lucky crouching nearby as he clambered over a fallen log toward the camp.

Lucky pounced. He slammed into Arrow's chest as the Fierce Dog hopped off the log, throwing him into a thicket of brambles. The young dog struggled, twisting beneath Lucky's weight, and Lucky pressed down onto his chest. Arrow gasped for breath but didn't bite or snap. The Fierce Dog looked exhausted.

There was no telling what he might do. Was Blade close? Lucky raised the alarm call. "Help! Intruder!" he barked.

The Packs burst out from their camp with a volley of high

barks. Sweet was in the lead. She took in the scene immediately, rushing to Lucky's side and pressing a paw down on the dog's throat.

"Who are you?" she snarled. "What are you doing here? Tell me at once or I'll rip your throat out!"

"Who cares what he says?" Moon barked. "We can't trust him. We should just kill him, or as soon as we release him he'll run back to his Pack."

"That's true." Sweet pressed harder on Arrow's throat, and Lucky saw the Fierce Dog wince. Her claws had drawn a trail of blood, which ran down his neck and dripped onto the fresh snow.

"Please don't kill me," he pleaded. "I've left Blade for good. I want to side with you."

"Didn't Fang say stuff like this when he tricked you, Lucky?" growled Bella.

"You can *never* trust a Fierce Dog," Bruno agreed.

"What about Storm?" Arrow yelped. "She's in your Pack—if you let me join, I'll prove that I can be trusted too."

"Storm is different," Snap insisted. "We've known her since she was a pup. Whereas you . . ." Her muzzle crinkled with distaste.

"Another spy sent by Blade," Lucky hissed, thumping Arrow

down harder against the bramble bush.

The Fierce Dog flinched. "I'm not a spy!"

Twitch loomed over him to snarl into one of his pointed ears. "Of course not. We'll just let you go and you won't harm us. You won't go straight back to Blade and tell her exactly where we are. How foolish of us to think the worst of you."

"Kill him now!" howled Breeze. Most of the other dogs were barking in agreement. Lucky glanced around at them as they pressed closer to Arrow, baring their fangs. Only Storm held back, her head cocked thoughtfully.

Sweet bore down on Arrow, and he yelped in a strangled voice, "I'm not a spy, I promise you! Blade already knows exactly where you are and what you've got planned."

Sweet loosened her grip slightly. "What do you mean?"

Arrow spoke breathlessly, spluttering out the words. "Your Omega," he gasped. "The strange little dog with the bulging eyes. He ran to Blade and told her you would come and deceive her. That you'd challenge her to a fight with Storm, but the rest of the Pack would be waiting to attack Blade and any Fierce Dog who comes with her. She knows everything, and she won't come alone—you can be sure of that!"

The little black dog hadn't been Omega since Sunshine had

taken over the role, but every dog in Sweet's Pack knew who Arrow meant.

"Whine," spat Lucky with disgust.

Sweet dropped her hold on Arrow's neck, and his head lolled back against the snow. "Watch him, Beta."

Lucky dipped his head in acknowledgment, keeping his forepaws on Arrow's chest. The Fierce Dog didn't struggle or try to rise. He lay in the mounting snow, panting.

Sweet and Twitch backed away a short distance, whispering to each other in lowered tones. Their Packs circled Lucky and Arrow, making sure the Fierce Dog was safely hemmed in.

Bruno snapped at the young dog's neck. "How did you know to find us here?"

"I told you, the small dog told Blade. All the Fierce Dogs heard it; the Pack was together. Every dog knows where you are. They're planning to surprise you with an attack. I wanted to warn you."

A tremor of fear rose through the Packs.

"The Fierce Dogs know where we are," whimpered Dart.

Whisper's eyes widened. "They'll be coming for us!"

"You should move," panted Arrow.

"Shut up, intruder!" snarled Bruno, and the young dog fell silent. No dog spoke for a while as the snow spun soundlessly down from the gray sky and fell on the leafless trees. *If Blade knows we're here, we'll have to go,* thought Lucky dejectedly. What would they do now?

Soon Sweet and Twitch returned, crunching over the fresh snow. The other dogs parted to let them through, and the Alphas sat at a short distance from Arrow.

Twitch was the first to speak. "We will hear what you have to say."

"But our agreeing to listen doesn't mean anything," Sweet was quick to add. "We don't see how we can trust you. But you'd better start talking."

Lucky drew back, allowing Arrow to roll onto his paws. Bruno, Bella, and Woody, the large thickset dog from Twitch's Pack, sat close to him, ready to pounce if he made a wrong move.

Arrow took a deep breath. For the most part he looked at Sweet and Twitch, though he glanced around at the other dogs. "I had to leave Blade's Pack," he began. "She's gone mad, always talking about her dreams and the death of the Earth-Dog. She said she predicted the second Growl, and she is desperate to kill Storm because she was born after the first Big Growl. She really believes that it's some sort of prophecy, that she *has* to kill pups born after the first Growl or Earth-Dog will finish her off." He appealed to Sweet. "You saw what she did to Fang. After he was so loyal to her! She thinks nothing of killing her own kind. If I'd been born just a few journeys of the Moon-Dog later, she would have killed me too."

Storm gave a low growl. "She's a monster."

Sweet's eyes were cool. "I thought you were supposed to be loyal to your Pack no matter what. Isn't that the Fierce Dog way?"

Arrow gave a small whine. "I hate betraying the dogs I've grown up with, but I can't go along with Blade. I had my doubts when she spoke about the Growl. I'd heard about what she'd done to Wiggle. But then I saw it—I saw her kill Fang with my own eyes. After that I couldn't be in her Pack anymore."

Lucky watched the Fierce Dog's dark eyes grow round. *I think he really means it. . . .*

"How do we know you're alone?" asked Twitch.

"I am, I promise. After what Blade did to Fang, I knew I had to go. I waited till I had my chance. Right after you came with your challenge, Blade sent me on a patrol with two other dogs, and when their backs were turned, I ran—and I haven't stopped running, not till I got here. Blade will kill me for sure if she catches me. And she won't be far behind, because she's coming for Storm."

Lucky's fur rose along his back.

Sweet's eyes still bored into the young Fierce Dog. "What do you know about her plans?"

"I know Blade is desperate to hunt down Storm—it's all she ever talks about. When Whine came to the camp a few nights ago, she couldn't believe her luck. He asked to join the Fierce Dogs in exchange for information. He *told* her your plan without any prompting. She knows you'll be hiding at the place with the high rocks. She'll be ready for you."

Lucky remembered his exchange with Blade that sunup. "She agreed to fight Storm—perhaps too easily. She didn't ask many questions." In hindsight, this struck him as odd. His tail drooped, and he gnawed at a bur in his paw. How had he been so easily fooled?

"What is she planning to do?" asked Twitch.

Arrow looked at him intently. "She won't give you the advantage. She'll lead her Pack through the longpaw town, but instead of taking them upstream along the riverbank, she will circle back through the forest and attack from behind, cornering you here, against the rocks. She expects you to be focused on the river path, so you won't be prepared for a rear attack. I came to warn you."

"I still don't understand *why* you would warn us," said Sweet flatly. "What's in it for you? If you think Blade's mad, why not just run away? Become a Lone Dog."

Lucky watched Arrow closely. The young Fierce Dog seemed to struggle in finding his words. "It didn't seem . . . *honorable* . . . that she would attack you like that. Despite our Alpha's orders, honor is important to a true Fierce Dog. We are not just savages." He looked up, carefully keeping his body in a submissive position, and Lucky saw his eyes lock with Storm's. Then he looked away again. "Anyway, I felt you should know." He added, in a quiet voice, "And I don't think I could manage as a Lone Dog. I've only ever known Pack life. I don't want to be alone."

Lucky felt a stab of pity for the Fierce Dog, remembering that he was only slightly older than Storm and couldn't have had an adult name for long. The snow swirled around Arrow thickly. Set aside from the other dogs, he looked isolated and strangely vulnerable, despite his muscular body and firm jaw.

Sweet caught Lucky's eye. "Whine left the Pack before Bella had the idea of approaching Twitch. I'm right, aren't I?"

Lucky thought a moment. He pictured the small dog disappearing into the sleet. Bruno had said a few words—something about it being a shame that Whine had left. The old dog had questioned how the Pack could ever defeat the Fierce Dogs, and it was only then that Bella had suggested approaching Twitch's

Pack. *Whine doesn't know about Twitch—which means that Blade can't know that we have other dogs prepared to fight alongside us.* He gave a quick dip of his head—Sweet was right.

Bella's eyes glittered. "That's true. Whine wasn't around when we spoke about Twitch's Pack."

"Well, that at least is good news," said Sweet. "This is going to come to a fight, one way or another. At least if we get moving now we'll keep some sort of advantage. I don't think it's an option to stick to the original plan—we can't just wait here for the Fierce Dogs to attack us."

Arrow sighed with relief. "You trust me?"

"I don't know," said Sweet. "But I believe that Blade knows our original plan to attack from the rocks. So we'll have to think of something else."

Lucky saw Whisper say something to Rake, who sidled up to Splash and murmured in his ear.

Splash padded toward Twitch respectfully, lowering his head. "Alpha, may I speak with you? Whisper has had an idea that I think might work."

Twitch and the rest of the dogs turned to look at the wiry black Beta. "Go ahead."

"If the Fierce Dogs are really going to cut through the forest, near our Pack's camp, there may be something we can do that would break up Blade's Pack and put them on the back paw. But it won't be easy." Splash shifted uneasily, looking about for a moment through the swirling snow. "Whichever dog takes on the mission, they will need to be fast. *Very* fast."

CHAPTER TWENTY

Lucky, Sweet, and Whisper padded through the snow. Already it was deep enough to cover Lucky's paws, concealing them beneath its cool white pelt. Flakes drifted through the sky, settling on the rocks, the trees, and the arching valley as the dogs wound a path inland, away from the riverbank. Lucky had seen snow in the city, but there the loudcages had smashed it beneath their spinning paws, and longpaws had trampled it underfoot.

Here, in a world without longpaws, there was no one to disturb the snow. It clung thickly to the land, and its icy touch reminded Lucky of Alfie. Lucky was haunted by the dead dog's words.

The Pack may still survive, as long as every dog does their duty when the Storm comes. Yours will be the most important of all.

Lucky frowned, stepping carefully through the snow. *But what is my duty?*

Sweet broke the silence. "Everything looks different in the snow." She glanced around, sniffing. "The river is behind us, but I don't remember the valley being so wide."

Lucky squinted through the swirling flakes. "The snow makes everything seem larger somehow."

"It's okay, I've lived near here all my life. I know exactly where we are," Whisper assured them in his soft voice. "Though we can't see it through the snow, the forest is right ahead of us and the longpaw town just a bit farther downstream." He peered over his right shoulder.

Lucky hoped the gray dog was right. The snow masked shapes, colors, and smells. "The snow changes everything."

Sweet's ears were pricked. "It's so quiet."

"Too cold for prey." Whisper started moving again. "A Pack of Fierce Dogs would stand out against the snow. If what Arrow said is true, they will have reached the town by now. They might have even started tracking the river or crossing through the forest."

Lucky shuddered. "You're right—we need to hurry."

They picked up their pace, slipping and crunching over the fresh snow until Lucky could just make out the outline of longpaw buildings and realized they had reached the outskirts of the town. A sharp scent caught his nose, and he stopped dead.

"Fierce Dogs!" he whined in a low voice. "They're close."

Whisper sniffed urgently, and Sweet pointed with her long, elegant muzzle. "There are paw tracks just up ahead." She approached cautiously, her tail straight out behind her. "All different sizes. It must be the whole Pack."

The hairs rose along Lucky's back. "Arrow was telling the truth. They're planning to take us by surprise. Whine must have told Blade our plan." Anger prickled his whiskers at the small dog's betrayal.

Sweet set her jaw. "That disloyal mutt thinks he's so clever, but he doesn't know *everything*."

Whisper blinked in acknowledgment. "You won't fight them alone."

"If we're lucky, we won't fight them at all." She gave the paw prints another sniff. "They must have left the town quite recently. These tracks won't last long in the snow."

Sweet was right. Already flakes were falling over the imprints of the Fierce Dogs' paws, masking them in white.

"This way," murmured Whisper, leading them away from the tracks and deeper into the valley. The brown trunks of trees emerged from the snow, the tops of their branches already white. The forest had been there all along!

Despite the cold, warmth unfurled in Lucky's chest, and he remembered his dream in which his pups had scampered beneath the Sun-Dog. Silently he thought of the Forest-Dog.

O wise Spirit Dog, you have always protected me. I need you now more than ever.

The dogs wove a path through the trees, stopping when they reached the entrance to a rock cave. Lucky and Sweet exchanged glances.

"What if the Fierce Dogs hear us?" Lucky asked.

A look of determination crossed Sweet's face. "We've come too far now to turn back." She threw back her head and started to howl. Lucky and Whisper joined in, barking as loud as they could by the mouth of the cave.

At first nothing happened. Lucky watched the cave, but as he barked he pictured the Fierce Dogs charging over the snow in formation, converging on the Wild Pack. He barked louder, straining his throat, risking a step closer to the cave.

A deep, furious roar emerged from the cave, and Lucky's heart skipped a beat. The dogs were shocked into silence, their eyes trained on the mouth of the cave.

Sweet seemed to come to her senses. "Keep barking!" she ordered.

All three dogs barked even more ferociously.

Lucky could feel the heavy thump of paws vibrating from the ground. Powdery snow slid off the top of the cave.

"She's coming," hissed Whisper, quaking with fear but continuing to bark.

"You can go now," Sweet told him.

"If you're sure . . . ?"

"Return to your Alpha. Run!" she ordered.

Whisper gave a brief nod and spun on his heels, bolting over the snow.

Lucky gave a long, powerful howl that drew all the breath from his lungs. He felt another thump from deep within the cave. The ground shook, and the giantfur burst out, her head twisting in a furious roar.

Sweet and Lucky backed away but kept barking.

The giantfur's red eyes darted from the dogs to the white forest, and she blinked in confusion at the snow. Then anger flashed across her face, and her lips peeled back. Drool slid off her jagged teeth. She lurched forward, rolled onto her back legs, and swiped at Lucky with a giant paw.

Lucky sprang back but kept barking. Fighting to control the terror that clutched at his belly, he did his best to provoke the beast. The giantfur roared again. Against the silent forest, the sound was like the thunder of the Sky-Dogs or the tearing growl of the Earth-Dog. Lucky's blood pulsed in his neck, and he gasped breathlessly, drawing back alongside Sweet.

"Ready?" she whispered.

Lucky flicked his ears in acknowledgment.

The giantfur rolled back onto her hind paws until she was standing like the trunk of a hefty tree. Both her forepaws flailed, cutting shapes in the air with their long, pointed claws.

"Now!" howled Sweet. She spun around and bolted, back toward the outskirts of the town. Lucky sprang after her. Risking a quick glance over his shoulder, he saw the giantfur hesitate, her brow furrowed in confusion. Then she charged, pounding over the snow with terrifying speed.

Lucky fought to keep up with the swift-dog, who seemed to be flying over the snow. It wasn't as easy for him. With his shorter legs and thicker frame, Lucky kept losing his footing, skidding, and colliding with twigs and debris concealed beneath the cool white mantle. He hadn't expected a beast the size of a giantfur to be able to run so fast.

By the time the dogs reached the Fierce Dogs' tracks, Lucky was fighting to keep up. The giantfur was still loping after them across the valley, kicking up clouds of snow.

"Can you see where they lead?" he panted.

"This way!" Sweet barked.

"I can't!" Lucky wheezed, sick with shame and terror as the giantfur charged toward them. "I won't make it!"

"There's a fence just up ahead. Jump behind it and hide—leave the giantfur to me!"

"I can't leave you!" he barked in panic. She was going to run straight into the Fierce Dog Pack!

"I'll be okay. I won't fight—with the Wind Dogs at my back, I can outrun any dog!"

A roar behind them made Lucky's heart leap to his throat. "But, Sweet—"

"The fence!" she snarled. "That's an order, Beta!"

With that, she sprang forward, sprinting across the snow and barking for the giantfur to follow. Lucky obeyed, his mind suddenly blank but his paws scrambling beneath him. He leaped the fence and collapsed in the snow, holding his breath so the giantfur wouldn't hear him. She paused beside the fence, panting and snorting. Sweet barked sharply, and Lucky heard the beast start to move again, her paws thumping heavily in the direction of Sweet's voice, thundering over the valley.

As the giantfur's heavy pawsteps faded, Lucky's breath exploded from his chest. He shook himself, gasping. Sense flooded back to him. He thought of Sweet, running alone toward the Fierce Dogs, that beast on her tail. He knew he should head back to the Pack—what if Whisper hadn't made it? What if something went wrong there and he was needed?

But he couldn't do it—he couldn't abandon Sweet. He sprang over the fence and started following the giantfur at a distance, advancing slowly. The beast's enormous tracks were impossible to miss, but despite the creature's size, Lucky could no longer see her through the swirling snow. Suddenly there was a shrill bark, and Lucky froze, ears pricked up. He could hear a commotion up ahead, the growl of the giantfur and the yelping of dogs.

He picked up his pace but was careful not to creep up too quickly behind the giantfur.

A Fierce Dog was barking in alarm. "Dogs! Quick! We're under attack!"

"What *is* it?" yelped another.

He heard Blade's panicked howl. "The swift-dog brought a snow monster! Take it down!"

Lucky crept low to the ground. He could just make out flashes of glossy fur between the flakes of spinning snow. There was no sign of Sweet—she must have bolted already, before Blade realized what was happening. The Fierce Dogs seemed to be falling into line, standing shoulder to shoulder. Then the giantfur charged toward them, a furious boulder of dark fur. A dog yelped in pain, and Lucky lowered his muzzle, crouching deep in the snow.

Guilt coursed through Lucky's fur. It was hard to hear the dog's whimpers. *Whatever I think about Blade, I helped lead the giantfur to the Fierce Dogs.*

"My leg! Help me, won't someone help me!"

An acid taste rose in Lucky's throat and he swallowed hard, feeling giddy.

"She's coming back!" It was Mace's voice.

Blade's desperate bark rang out over the valley. "Stop her before she kills us all! Go for her flanks and haunches! Once we bring her down, we can reach her filthy throat!"

Lucky heard the thump of bodies colliding. The giantfur roared indignantly. There was a heavy pounding of paws and an agonized yowl. Lucky buried his head beneath his paws. He wished he could block his ears. Over the stillness of the snowy valley it was impossible to miss the sounds of teeth tearing flesh, of jaws crunching bone. A dog was wheezing desperately, gurgling and spitting, and a sharp smell rose on the cold, gray air. The metallic scent of blood.

When Lucky scrambled through the forest to arrive at the rocky outcrop, he was panting so hard that he struggled to breathe. Heat pulsed through his body, despite the biting snow. The white pelt lay so heavy over the rocks that they had the soft, smooth appearance of skin. But underneath the icy flakes, Lucky knew that the hardstone was rigid and unforgiving. He let out an anxious whimper. There was no sign of his Pack. He padded around the rocks, scratching at the snow with a forepaw. The rush of a rich, delicious smell touched his nose. *Sweet!*

She had left a trail down to the riverbank. He circled the outcrop, weaving between the trees, and he found the path to the water's edge. Ice stretched over the surface, shiny and deadly.

An angry bark rang through the air. "Who is it? Identify yourself!" A figure stepped out from behind the rocks, hackles up and head dropped in challenge.

Lucky knew that voice. "Mickey? It's me!" He ran to the black-and-white dog, tail lashing.

Immediately Mickey morphed from a ferocious guard-dog

into something resembling an eager pup. He growled gently, covering Lucky with nips and nudges. "Sweet got back a while ago. You took so long! We thought something terrible had happened to you. They'll all be so relieved to see you." He started along the snowy bank and dipped between some trees. The two Packs were gathered together, and they yipped excitedly as Mickey and Lucky appeared.

Sweet rushed to greet Lucky, licking his nose and nuzzling his neck. "Our plan worked perfectly," she told him. "The giantfur attacked the Fierce Dogs, and they weren't ready for it at all. I left them in chaos and ran full pelt to the Packs. Some of Blade's dogs gave chase, but none of them could catch me and they soon gave up." Her eyes glinted with satisfaction.

"Was Blade hurt?" asked Lucky.

Sweet let out a puff of breath. "Honestly I'm not sure—it was madness when the giantfur attacked her Pack, and I didn't hang around to see what happened."

Storm nudged her way between Martha and Moon. A shadow crossed her eyes. "I hope Blade died in agony. It's no more than she deserves," she spat.

The ferocity of Storm's words unsettled Lucky. "I heard some of the clash," he murmured. "I couldn't see anything, though.

Several dogs were whining. Another dog was howling in pain. But I don't think it was Blade." He gazed over the snowcapped land. It was eerily quiet. "Blade saw you, Sweet. She knows you led the giantfur to her Pack. If she's alive, she'll be desperate for revenge." He tried to forget the sounds of mauling and chomping, and the howls of injured attack-dogs.

Sweet's voice was low. "We will have to fight them on open ground. Hopefully they'll have lost the advantage that Whine gave them, and they won't know about Twitch's Pack."

"But Blade will be angrier than ever," Dart murmured, creeping close to Bruno's side.

Sweet didn't answer. "There isn't much time." She led Lucky, Twitch, and Splash a short distance from the others. "I will need your help to rally the dogs." Then she spoke up, so that every dog could hear her. "My Pack, Twitch's Pack, the time has come to fight together, shoulder to shoulder. The Fierce Dogs are coming. They will be angry and bent on revenge. Above all, Blade will have riled them up and made them believe that the only way to prevent another, final Growl is to kill Storm. We must not allow them to break our defenses. We must combat our fear and fight bravely. We have come at last to the Storm of Dogs, but we will be triumphant."

A series of barks rose in agreement, but Lucky could also sniff the tang of fear-scent in the air. Following orders, he busied himself urging the stronger fighters to the front of the Pack. Mickey, Snap, and Bruno came forward. At Twitch's encouragement, his best fighters joined them.

Sweet paced between the ranks, tall and proud on her slender legs. "I want you to stay close to one another when the Fierce Dogs arrive. If we separate, it's easier for them to pick us off or break through our defenses." She nudged Dart away from the edge of the riverbank with her muzzle. "And watch out for the water. The ice will be thin—if you tumble off the bank, it could crack and you'll end up in the freezing water. I don't think even Martha would last long down there."

The black water-dog cocked her head in acknowledgment and Dart shuddered, moving even farther away from the edge of the bank.

Lucky watched uneasily as Arrow edged toward the front of the Pack, pressing between Bruno and Bella. The Fierce Dog dropped his muzzle, his eyes focused dead ahead.

Lucky couldn't help thinking about Fang, who had been loyal to Blade despite her cruel treatment, and who had helped her trick the Wild Pack and hold Lucky prisoner. *In the name of the Sky-Dogs, who watch over everything—please let our faith in Arrow be justified.*

He snapped out of his thoughts to see Storm muscling forward, shoving Rake out of the way in her eagerness to reach the front of the Pack.

Sweet glared at her sternly. "Not you."

"But I *have* to!" she protested. "Blade wouldn't even be coming here if it wasn't for me. I *must* be in the battle. I may be the best fighter we have, and I need revenge for my litter-brothers."

"And you will have it," said Lucky. "But you can't be too exposed. For now, we need you to hold back."

Storm's floppy ears twitched, but she made no move to retreat.

"Beta told you to hold back—*do it!*" Sweet barked.

With heavy steps, as though her paws were made of hardstone, Storm turned around and plodded a few rows back. She sat with a sulky droop of her ears and brooded while dogs arranged themselves around her. Lucky felt a warm glow in his chest. Storm was still so pup-like—he remembered her boisterous enthusiasm in the days after he and Mickey had found her, and the sorrow that followed a telling off. She hadn't changed.

Martha padded up to Storm and rested her head on the Fierce Dog's shoulder. "It's okay, young dog," she murmured. "You're safer back here."

"But I don't want to be *safe*—I want to fight for my Pack, like everyone else."

Martha's voice was soothing. "Your time will come."

Lucky watched as Storm buried her head against Martha's thick black coat. It was as though no bitterness had ever developed between the two dogs. He noticed the water-dog's gentle affection, so like that of a Mother-Dog, and the trust in Storm's dark face.

Satisfied that Storm would stay toward the rear of the Pack—at least for now—Lucky stalked along the riverbank, checking that all of the dogs were fit and ready to fight. Most of them had grown bolder, buoyed by one another's enthusiasm. But when Lucky reached the back of the group, he saw that Sunshine was in a state. The little dog trembled in fear, her dark eyes worried. Her head craned over the snow and every sound made her spook, spinning on her paws, breathing quickly.

Lucky licked her ears and spoke soothingly. "How are you feeling?" Sunshine puffed up her chest and tried to look fierce, but her shaking hackles betrayed her terror. "I will do my best to fight for my Pack," she said bravely.

"I don't want you to fight. You're small and white; you can

barely be seen in the snow. I want you to hide and stay safe."

"But then I'd be a coward," she whimpered. "I have to do my duty."

"A dog's duty may come in different forms," Lucky assured her. "Yours is not to fight. Stay safe now—you help the Pack in other ways." He lowered his voice. "When Sweet led the giantfur to the Fierce Dogs, I had to hide behind a fence. I wasn't fast enough to help Sweet, and I felt terrible about that. But every dog is different—we contribute according to our own unique skills. You help to keep up our morale. That is more valuable than big jaws or sharp claws. That is the most important job of all."

She blinked at him gratefully, and her body relaxed. With a small wag of the tail, she backed away from the other dogs, toward a mound of fresh snow at the base of the tree. There she dug herself a hiding place and shuffled deep within the mound, disappearing in a bundle of white.

Lucky returned to stand by Sweet's side at the front of the Pack. It was hard to see more than a few dog-lengths ahead. The snow was falling more heavily, the air a blizzard of thick white flakes. A deep chill ran through Lucky's bones. This was it—the Storm of Dogs he had pictured in his dreams—here at last.

His words to Sunshine echoed in his ears. *A dog's duty may come in different forms.*

But what was his duty? What was the role that Alfie spoke of? And when the time came, would he know what to do?

CHAPTER TWENTY-ONE

It was impossible to tell the time of day. Lucky gazed at the sky, but all he could see was a swirling haze of white. The Sun-Dog might have gone to sleep by now, warm and safe beyond Ice Wind's freezing grasp, but there was no sign of the Moon-Dog. *Could they have both deserted us?* Lucky wondered. No, that wasn't possible. His Mother-Dog had told him that when the Sun-Dog retreated to his den, the Moon-Dog appeared to watch over dogs. That way, there was always a Spirit Dog with an eye to the world below, keeping dogs safe.

Mother lived in different times, thought Lucky sadly. *When longpaws controlled the city . . . when the Earth-Dog was peaceful and on our side.*

That world had gone.

He shivered, trying to rid his fur of the thick white flakes, but they just kept coming. Sweet stood very still at his flank, squinting through the snow. Twitch was sitting on her other side, his sensitive ears alert for sound and his nostrils pulsing.

"Anything?" asked Sweet.

The floppy-eared dog sighed. "Not yet."

There was a murmur of disquiet from the Wild Packs gathered behind them. Lucky longed for a bird to shrill, or a mouse to scamper along the riverbank—anything to interrupt the creepy silence.

What's taking the Fierce Dogs so long? Could it be possible that the giantfur had killed *all* of Blade's Pack? Or that the beast had scared them so badly that they'd chosen to run away?

Then Lucky picked up the faintest sound—the soft crunch of a paw in snow. Brittle fear caught at the back of his throat. Sweet tensed, and Twitch's head rose sharply. They had heard it too.

There passed a long moment when all they could hear was the whisper of snow as it spun from the sky and fell to earth. Then there was another crunch of paws, and a dark shape loomed out of the blizzard.

Blade's eyes were bloodshot, and her lip quivered with rage. But her muscles flexed, and there was no sign of injury beneath her glossy fur. She scanned the Wild Dogs, her lip crinkling with disgust, as her deputies, Mace and Dagger, appeared behind her.

A jagged wound ran along Mace's cheek and the fur hung off his shoulder, revealing a hunk of skin as pink as a dog's tongue. Lucky shuddered. The giantfur must have done that. . . .

Behind the deputies, Lucky could just make out the silhouettes of other Fierce Dogs. He couldn't tell how many through the swirling blizzard, but he thought it might be fewer now after the Fierce Dogs' battle with the giantfur.

"You!" snarled Blade, her red eyes locking onto Sweet. "Swift-dog! I saw you run past before the ice monster attacked. You led her to us. It was your wicked plan."

Sweet's face was tight with tension. "And I would do it again."

Blade thumped one dark paw on the snow, sending up a cloud of white. "That trick shows you for the cowards you are, and so does your filthy plot to ambush us by the rocks. Your Pack is too weak to fight us in open combat. I hope you will continue to be cowards. Hand over Storm—she belongs to me."

"My Pack has been joined by another," Sweet growled. "Twitch is a brave fighter, and his dogs stand alongside mine."

Blade took in the floppy-eared dog, her eyes widening with surprise. She snorted in amusement. "Swift-dog, I knew you were weak, but I had no idea you were *that* desperate! A cripple? Leading a Pack?"

Mace and Dagger barked with cruel amusement. Lucky felt anger replace fear, gushing hotly through his limbs, but Twitch did not respond. Instead he watched Blade with a sort of cool detachment. It seemed to unnerve her, and she ran her tongue over her muzzle.

Blade's eyes trailed across the frozen river, and her voice became grave. "There isn't much time. I predicted another Growl, and it came. In my dreams last night the Spirit Dogs warned of a third and final Growl. Earth-Dog will perish and night will fall, perhaps forever." She met Lucky's eye. "The City Rat knows. He has seen it too."

A bolt of fire shot between them, like Lightning's flame. Lucky could hardly breathe. *I never told her about my dreams. How does she know?* Had Whine told her?

Blade gave him a curious look and shifted her attention back to Sweet. "The blood of the pup is needed to appease Earth-Dog. Another Growl is coming. I know the City Rat can feel it—but can't the rest of you? Only Storm's death will stop it."

Lucky felt a strange tingling in his fur, a familiar agitation. Beyond the twisting snow, the air seemed to tremble. His hackles rose, and the fur along his spine felt frozen like whiskers of ice. He rebuked himself. *It's a trick. She's got me imagining things. She probably knows about my dreams from Whine. Sweet shared them with the Pack, and now Blade's trying to scare us into giving up Storm.* He took a deep breath, his hackles rising.

Sweet showed no sign of fear. "We will defend Storm and our territory with our lives. There are more of us now, with Twitch's Pack fighting alongside us. He is a brave, honorable Alpha, and his dogs are fierce in battle. There are fewer of you since your tussle with the giantfur. You are greatly outnumbered."

Lucky admired Sweet's determination. He knew her words about Pack numbers would encourage the Wild Dogs.

And she wasn't done yet.

"Your Pack has been bullied and oppressed under your leadership," said Sweet. "Many witnessed the savagery with which you murdered Fang, a pup who was ever loyal to you. Some have had enough." She nodded at Arrow, and the young Fierce Dog stepped forward.

Lucky held his breath. *If Arrow is going to betray us, now would be the time. . . .*

But to Lucky's intense relief, Blade's ears shot back as she saw Arrow approach, and she spat with rage. "You traitor!" she howled. "I will tear you limb from limb."

"If he doesn't kill you first," Sweet snarled.

Blade took a step closer, hackles high and lips curled back. Mace and Dagger flanked her and other Fierce Dogs stepped forward, taking position. Lucky could see his former Alpha's wolfish outline near the back and felt a pang of anger.

Blade glared at Sweet with contempt. "Don't you get it yet? You may have more dogs, you may play more tricks. But we are natural fighters, while your pathetic Pack is nothing more than a band of rejects—a bunch of Wild Dogs without dignity or discipline and the lame, weak, and cowardly runts that the longpaws left behind. We are trained and prepared. We were born to kill, and we will destroy every one of you."

The Fierce Dogs snarled and barked in agreement as a creeping dread ran along Lucky's back. Some of the Wild Dogs had never killed anything larger than a rabbit. He thought of Daisy, of Moon's pups. . . .

He hid his fear, barking at Blade. "Enough talk! You have heard our Alpha: We will not give Storm to you to slay in cold blood. We are *not* scared of you. Our dogs are ready to fight to the end."

A clamor of growls and barks leaped from the Wild Pack. The Fierce Dogs answered with their own furious snarls.

Sweet's voice rang out over the baying dogs, crisp and clear on the freezing air.

"Wild Dogs: Attack!"

The dogs charged, kicking up clouds of snow beneath their paws. Sweet ran straight at Blade, and for an instant Lucky saw a look of shock cross the Fierce Dog's face. She clearly hadn't expected the Wild Dogs to make the first move. Then Blade's jaw hardened, and she shrieked, "Kill, Fierce Dogs, *kill!*"

A tremor of panic rose among the two Packs massed along the riverbank as the attack-dogs charged out of the snow. Some had been badly injured by the giantfur, but this only seemed to make them more determined. There were fewer Fierce Dogs, but Blade was right—they were trained fighters. They held their ranks as they advanced on Sweet's and Twitch's Packs, their eyes filled with fury.

The Fierce Dogs slammed into the Wild Dogs with brutal force. Dagger went straight for Arrow, throwing the young dog against a tree and snapping long sharp teeth at his neck.

"Filthy traitor!" rasped the huge Fierce Dog. "You'll see what we do to your kind."

Lucky was about to run to Arrow's aid when he caught a flash of gray fur out of the corner of his eye, just before Snap yowled in pain. The half wolf had slunk behind the Fierce Dogs, taking his former Packmate by surprise and sinking his long jaws into her back leg. Snap fought wildly, scratching her former Alpha's face, but she couldn't shake herself free.

"We were in the same Pack!" Snap gasped. "I followed your orders—I was loyal to you."

"Your loyalty means nothing," the dog-wolf snarled, biting harder.

Mickey bounded out of the blizzard, catching their old Alpha off guard with a thrust from his forepaws. The half wolf released his grip on Snap's leg and rolled onto his side. "Leashed Rat!" he spluttered angrily. "I never knew you could fight." He sprang up and made to lunge, but in a flash of pale fur, Sweet appeared from nowhere to put her sleek body between the half wolf and the Farm Dog.

Alpha's lips curled in a cruel smirk. "So you're the dog who took my place?" he growled. "You're the new me?"

Sweet's spine stiffened as a deep rumble sounded in her chest. "I'm nothing like you," she snarled. "You were *never* a true Alpha!"

Then she charged at the dog-wolf, bundling him to the icy ground and sinking a deep bite into the dog-wolf's hackles. As the two of them rolled over and over, snapping and snarling, Mickey stayed close, ready to come to his leader's aid.

But I don't think Sweet will need any help now.

Lucky's attention snapped back to Arrow. The young Fierce Dog was whimpering as Dagger pinned him to the ground with his sturdy forepaws. Blood gushed from Arrow's ear, which Dagger had torn. Arrow bucked and strained, but he couldn't get free, and he was barking in alarm.

Lucky started toward him. *The young dog has proven his loyalty to Sweet's Pack. He deserves our help; he's a Wild Dog now.* "Hold on!"

"Going somewhere?" It was Mace, Blade's Beta. His thick, muscular body blocked Lucky's way. Arrow was still barking for backup, but there was nothing Lucky could do. He tried to slip past Mace, but the Fierce Dog was quick, despite his bulk. He sprang at Lucky, snapping and snarling with spit on his teeth.

The dogs tussled, Lucky bucking and leaping out of Mace's reach. Bruno came to Lucky's aid, baring his teeth and snarling, but even together they could hardly fend off the Fierce Dog's frenzied attack. Mace was bearing down on them, shoving them back toward the river.

Another panicked howl rose from Arrow.

Lucky saw a flash of sandy fur dart toward the tree where Dagger had pinned the young dog down. It was Bella! She launched herself at Dagger, smashing his head against the tree with a powerful thump of her hind legs.

Arrow twisted out of the Fierce Dog's grip. He planted himself at Bella's side as Dagger rose shakily to his paws.

A searing pain flashed through Lucky's leg, and his gaze shot back to Mace. Blade's deputy had taken advantage of Lucky's lapse of attention, ripping open the scar along Lucky's leg where the dog-wolf had gouged out a chunk of flesh in the cave. The smell of blood filled the air, and Lucky staggered, giddy with pain. His pulse thrummed in his ears, and his throat was dry as sand. For a moment, the land grew dim, as though the snow had melted and the Sun-Dog had vanished for good.

A volley of frenzied barks caught Lucky's ears, and he came to his senses. Mace was on the ground, pinned by a mass of dogs. Lucky spotted Whisper's damaged gray tail. He made out the figures of Bruno, Rake, and Moon alongside him, beneath the spinning snow. They pressed against Mace, holding him back. Lucky regained his balance, heartened by how bravely the two Wild Packs fought side by side. *Maybe we can beat Blade's Pack after all....*

As Lucky dragged himself through the snow, he stumbled over something tough and heavy as a tree trunk. A Fierce Dog lay on her side, her eyes wide open and her pink tongue lolling between her jaws. Blood oozed from deep gouges in her belly.

The battle's first death.

Lucky didn't know the dog's name. Sorrow tingled through his fur. *Why did we have to fight? No dog should die like this.* He reminded himself that the Fierce Dogs had brought the battle to them. *We didn't want this.*

He licked the wound on his leg and looked out over the bloody scene by the riverbank. The dogs were fighting savagely, a swirl of colorful pelts in a blizzard of snow. The world was turning from white to red, the metallic tang of blood rising thickly. It was just like his visions. Worse . . . it was real, and it was happening to his friends. His family.

A whine rose from farther up the riverbank, and Lucky leaped up with a grimace, tensed to attack. He crept forward, blinking through the snow. Whisper was trapped between two Fierce Dogs. The skinny gray dog spun back and forth, trying to face them down while protecting his delicate flanks. His attackers slunk closer, their teeth bared. Whisper would be butchered! Forgetting the pain in his leg, Lucky crashed toward the closest Fierce Dog with a growl.

At the same moment, Storm pounced at the other attack-dog, knocking him down and biting his neck. She sank in her fangs and shook wildly, as though she was throttling a rabbit. The Fierce

Dog's eyes bulged and his mouth moved, but the only sound that emerged was a gurgling whimper. Blood spurted from the wound at his throat, and Storm pulled back. The Fierce Dog beneath her was dead.

The dog Lucky had tackled struggled away from him, watching Storm with shock and fear. "Storm is unstoppable," she gasped. "We cannot win this fight!" The huge black-and-tan dog shrank away and vanished into the swirling whiteness, her tail clinging to her flank.

Storm turned away from the dead Fierce Dog to speak to Whisper. "Are you okay?"

Lucky felt a burst of pride in the young dog. She was bold and fearless, a true warrior, but with a Wild Dog's loyalty to her own Pack.

Whisper gazed at Storm in awe. "Praise the Sky-Dogs! You saved me again!"

A howl of grief rose on the freezing air. Lucky spun around and made for the rocky outcrop with Storm and Whisper beside him, their paws slipping on sludge dyed red with blood. Even the sky had taken on a red tinge. The snow spinning against it looked ghoulish in the low light.

Lucky's eyes trailed the jagged rocks, trying to find the source of the cry. Then he spotted Chase, the small ginger dog from Twitch's Pack, shaking at the bottom of the rocks. Next to her lay Splash. Great bite marks appeared along the Beta's foreleg, and part of his lip had been torn from his face. Even in death, it looked as though he was snarling, his teeth exposed in the bleeding gums.

Lucky recoiled as bile rose in his throat. Chase looked up at him. The small dog's body was shaking so hard that her words were half-garbled. "B-b-b-lade," she managed. "She . . . she k-killed him!"

Blade's silky voice emerged from the snow. "And I'd do it again."

Chase made a break for her, trying to scramble up the rocks, and Lucky threw himself in the way. "No!" he barked sharply. The small dog's grief would get her killed.

Blade took a threatening step toward Lucky, glaring at him furiously. "At last I get to pick off the City Rat." She pressed back on her haunches, preparing to pounce. Lucky's heart pumped violently. His leg was bleeding, and his head felt light. He wouldn't have the strength to fight her off.

For a moment he thought of the Forest-Dog, and the stillness of the woods in the snow. *You have always protected me. If you can work a miracle, wise Spirit Dog, please save me one more time.*

There was a dull thump overhead and a boulder tumbled from the rock face, smashing down in front of Blade's paws. She sprang back, panicked. Suddenly she was a different dog—wild-eyed with fear. "The Growl!" she gasped. "It's coming!"

The fighting paused as the dogs froze where they stood, their bodies heaving.

"Is it the Growl?" yipped Dart in terror.

"The Earth-Dog is angry!" barked Dagger.

The Fierce Dogs started barking, and some of the Wild Dogs joined in, crazed with fear. Lucky nudged Chase away from Blade. When they were safely beyond the grasp of her fangs, Lucky stopped, sniffing the air. He sensed no vibrations. The ground felt steady beneath his paws. *Did the Forest-Dog hear my words?* He peered through the snow at the top of the rocky outcrop. *Could that be . . . ?* A bundle of snow seemed to shift between the rocks, scampering out of sight. *Not the Forest-Dog—Sunshine!*

He remembered what he'd told her: *A dog's duty may come in different forms. But what is my duty?* he wondered again.

Blade seemed to jolt out of her panic. "The rats are getting away!" she boomed. "Stop them!"

At once the Fierce Dogs fell into line, hurtling toward the Wild Pack with deadly ferocity. The battle started again in a whirl of snow and blood. Snap and Mickey fought back-to-back, protecting each other but surrounded. Bruno was badly wounded.

The old dog fought on, though he could barely drag his hind legs and his face was twisted in pain. Twitch was fighting with vigor, snapping viciously with his teeth and rearing up onto his back legs to swipe at a Fierce Dog with his good front paw, but the strain was showing in his exhausted body.

Fear clutched at Lucky's throat, and his breath came in fast gulps. The Fierce Dogs were overwhelming them. He was thrust to one side as Storm tore past him, racing along the waterfront.

He sprang after her. "Storm? Storm, what's wrong?"

Then Lucky saw it: Their old Alpha and two Fierce Dogs had converged on Martha at the edge of the frozen river. They snapped and wrenched at her flanks and she stumbled, struggling to keep her footing. Great clumps of her long black fur were sinking onto the bloodstained sludge.

"Bring her down!" snarled one of the Fierce Dogs, and the half wolf smashed his shoulder into Martha's side. The two Fierce Dogs mauled her flanks, their muzzles soaked with blood. The black dog couldn't defend herself against such a vicious attack. One hind leg collapsed behind her, and the Fierce Dogs barked in triumph.

"Get away from her!" howled Storm. She sprang onto the wolf-dog's back, sinking her teeth into his neck, so wild with rage that the Fierce Dogs shrank back. Storm bit harder, releasing a dark

SURVIVORS: STORM OF DOGS

river of blood that splattered onto the dirty snow. The half wolf shook himself free with a shrill whine and fled after the Fierce Dogs.

"Coward!" growled Lucky.

"I'll kill him!" Storm shrieked.

Lucky placed a gentle paw on her flank. "Martha's in trouble. . . ."

The great black dog had slumped onto her belly and was wheezing badly. Blood sprang from the deep bites in her flanks. She sank her head between her forepaws, resting it on the earth. A calmness seemed to come over her, and her breathing eased.

Then her eyes met Lucky's, and her floppy black ears pricked up. "Where's Storm?" she gasped. "Is she okay?"

Storm's eyes were full of fear. She crouched in the snow, her muzzle close to Martha's face. "I'm here."

The great black dog licked Storm's whiskers. "That's good," she murmured in her deep, soothing voice. "You have grown up to be so strong and courageous. We are all so proud of you."

Storm no longer looked like a deadly attack-dog. She seemed to shrink before Lucky's eyes, turning into the fragile pup called Lick, eager to prove herself, yearning for love. "It's only because you believe in me," she whined.

Martha's eyes sparkled. "Continue to be loyal—to be the strong and kind dog I know you are."

"I learned that from you," Storm told her. "You have always been like a Mother-Dog to me. I need you here, I need you to remind me."

"You don't need reminding. The strength and kindness are in you." Martha's eyes began to close.

Lucky quivered with sadness, an ache tightening in his throat. He watched helplessly as panic crossed Storm's face and she nudged the great dog with her nose.

Martha opened her eyes slowly. Her voice was light as the swirling snow. "I'll be with River-Dog now, I will be free . . . and I will always watch over you and the rest of the Pack." Her tail gave a jerk and settled on the snow as her eyes fell shut for the final time.

With a piercing howl, Storm leaped to her paws. "This is Blade's doing! Her fault, all of it!" Before Lucky could stop her, she had spun around and leaped over the edge of the bank. She landed on the frozen river, sliding out into the center on braced legs. Her eyes were furious, her hackles high. "Where are you, Blade, you pathetic coward? Come and face me, if you dare!"

CHAPTER TWENTY-TWO

The dogs rushed to the riverbank. The Fierce and Wild Packs snapped and snarled at each other, but the real fighting stopped as they jostled to see Storm. Thorn started climbing over the edge, onto the frozen ice.

"We'll help!" she yapped.

Beetle scrambled after her. "You don't need to fight alone!"

"I do," Storm barked. "Get back on the bank—*please*. I know you mean well, but this isn't your battle."

Reluctantly the young dogs turned and climbed back onto the snowcapped bank, where Moon was waiting anxiously.

Lucky squeezed a path between the Packs. "The ice . . . it could crack! You don't have to do this, Storm!"

Storm showed no hint of fear. She stood glaring at the bank.

"I *do* have to, Lucky," she replied. "It's time to settle this fight, once and for all."

Blade sauntered along the riverbank, ignoring Martha's prone body. Her eyes were fixed on Storm. "Finally the pup has the honor to confront me. I thought you would try to run away forever."

A hush fell over the dogs lined up along the bank.

Storm's muzzle wrinkled. "I have been longing for this moment. It is time for you to pay for what you did to my litter-brothers—time to avenge Martha, my Mother-Dog, and all the other dogs you killed without a moment of remorse."

Blade took a step onto the frozen river. The ice creaked beneath her paw, and Lucky's ears flicked back as he wondered if it would hold her weight. It must have been frozen solid—it held fast as Blade crept closer to Storm until the two Fierce Dogs were squared up to each other.

Blade made the first move. She lunged at Storm and their bodies slammed together. The two dogs skidded on the ice and rolled into a frenzied tussle. The dogs along the bank started barking and snarling, calling out support for Storm or Blade.

Lucky pressed his forepaws deep into the snowy bank, his

whole body throbbing with tension. The sky was silvery, and the snow was still falling so hard that it was difficult to see what was happening. Blade had pushed Storm down onto the ice and was bearing down on her, snapping at her face. Then Storm scrambled free, sliding over the ice and tripping Blade off her hind legs with the swipe of a paw so the bigger dog fell with a thud.

Lucky's ears pricked up. He'd spotted a flash of a familiar gray pelt stalking through the snow by the rocky outcrop. *What's our old Alpha up to?*

As Lucky watched, the dog-wolf looped through a patch of heavy snowfall along a ridge of rock, approaching the edge of the frozen river farther downstream. *He's trying to creep up on Storm and Blade.*

The other dogs hadn't noticed, focusing on the fight ahead. At this distance, the dog-wolf was almost invisible through the blizzard, but Lucky could make out a faint movement of gray fur as the half wolf edged closer to the tussle, keeping low to the ground.

With a vicious jerk of her head, Storm ripped off one of Blade's pointed ears. Blade howled in pain and head-butted Storm, sending the young dog spinning across the ice toward the rocks.

Suddenly the dog-wolf leaped from the rocks onto Storm's back, angling his long muzzle to bite down on her throat.

Lucky's world froze as he stared from the riverbank. Blade was rearing on the ice, Storm buckling beneath the half wolf's grip. In that instant, no dog moved. Even the snow seemed to stop falling, each flake suspended and glinting like clear-stone. Terror surged through Lucky. *This isn't how it's supposed to be!* The final battle between Blade and Storm would be cut short—the young dog would fall because of a cowardly attack. Martha and Splash would have died for nothing.

Blade will win the Storm of Dogs.

A light seemed to rise through the icy air, the last sparkle of the Sun-Dog outlining the trees of the forest. *He was there all along— the Spirit Dogs never deserted us.* Clarity came to Lucky. He knew what he had to do.

This *is my duty.*

The dogs along the bank were barking again, the snow was falling, and their old Alpha was peeling back his lips, preparing to bite. In an instant Lucky was flying over the edge of the bank, skidding onto the ice. He threw all his weight against his old Alpha, knocking the half wolf off Storm's back. The Storm of Dogs would be a fair fight—whatever happened now.

The wolf-dog landed hard but rolled back to his feet, spitting with anger. "City Rat! Will I never be rid of you?" He lunged at Lucky's injured leg, but Lucky threw himself forward, fighting harder than he had in his life. His teeth snapped feverishly until he found flesh. He bit hard, then drew back before the dog-wolf could strike, starting forward, then ducking away, doing his best to confuse his opponent.

The dog-wolf's eyes flashed. "I am stronger than you. I will win, and you will die out here on the ice, far from your city and your begging and tricks."

Anger flared in Lucky's heart. *He wants tricks? I'll show him tricks!* As the half wolf started to rush forward, Lucky gave a yelp and folded onto one side. He whimpered, cringing away from the dog-wolf. He heard the Wild Pack barking desperately.

Mickey's voice rose over the other dogs. "Leave him alone! This isn't fair!"

"Not even fit to fight," the half wolf mocked.

Lucky, seeing him drop his guard, sprang forward, sinking his teeth into the dog-wolf's flank and biting down with all his might. "Fitter than you think!" Lucky snarled as he released and lunged again.

The old Alpha howled in shock and pain. He struggled to get up, but his long legs skidded and he fell, striking his head on the ice.

He tried to rise again, but his feet slid, and he fell back upon the ice. Lucky stood over him, and the dog-wolf cowered. "Mercy," he begged, his voice cracking. "I should never have sided with the Fierce Dogs. Don't kill me!"

The dogs along the bank were barking wildly. Most of their words were lost in the ruckus, but Lucky heard Bella's voice. "You can't trust him!"

Lucky hesitated. The dog-wolf didn't deserve his compassion, but he looked so pitiful, collapsed on the ice. Lucky felt the rage drain from his body. He shook his fur and narrowed his eyes. "Run away and never show your face again, not here, or our camp, not in the forest or by the banks of the Endless Lake. If you promise to disappear for good, I will let you live."

"I promise!" the half wolf spluttered. "You won't see me again." He struggled to his paws and turned to go. Lucky sighed deeply, then remembered Storm and turned to see that she and Blade were fighting again. Through the tumbling snow they were a blur of dark pelts, their blood vivid red on the ice.

Then pain tore through Lucky's shoulder. Lucky gasped with shock—the dog-wolf had bitten down into his flesh. Lucky spun sharply, throwing his opponent over his shoulder.

His old Alpha crashed against the ice with a snapping sound, his head rolling at a strange angle. He lay still, and after a moment of hesitation—was this another trick?—Lucky moved forward to sniff at the half wolf. His neck had broken on impact . . . he was dead.

Lucky dropped back. A memory of Alfie's killing flashed through his mind. The Pack's former Alpha had brought the small dog down without a second thought. Now the half wolf lay broken and bleeding on the ice. *Is that what Alfie meant in my dream, that his death put us on this course . . . ?* Alfie's death had set Lucky against the half wolf. Ever since that moment, the two of them had been destined to fight—and now their fight was over.

Lucky limped slowly back over the ice. Exhaustion shuddered through him, and he'd hardly reached the bank before he slid onto a heap of snow, panting breathlessly as he watched the sparring Fierce Dogs. He longed to help Storm, but even if he could have, he knew they had to fight it out. He felt someone licking the gouge in his flank, and he winced.

Bella blinked down at him, her face tight with concern. "You're going to be okay, Yap." She returned to the wound, licking it carefully.

"Thanks, Squeak," he murmured, using her pup name, just as she had used his. He felt light-headed, rabbit paws scrambling between his ears. He dared not take his eyes off Blade and Storm. He had to focus. . . .

"Earth-Dog must have blood!" Blade barked.

Storm raised her head proudly, red staining her teeth. "You're wrong! This has nothing to do with Earth-Dog! You claim to be in touch with the Spirit Dogs, to speak for them. You're not a prophet—you're just a mad bully." She reared back onto her hind legs like a giantfur, her eyes wild. "I am the true daughter of Earth-Dog and River-Dog. Earth-Dog has seen plenty of blood already. She has had enough—we have *all* had enough!" With that, Storm slammed down her forepaws.

The sound of cracking ice silenced the baying dogs along the edges of the riverbank. The ice broke, shattering like clear-stone, and both Fierce Dogs plummeted into the river with a mighty splash.

Lucky shuffled to the edge of the ice, followed by Bella, as dogs yelped around him. Below, Lucky could see dark shapes fighting in the freezing water. He held his breath, his head thumping with pain. One dark body was sinking, sending up plumes of blood. The other dog was rising to the surface—but who was it? Was it Blade's larger form, her wild eyes, coming back? Lucky's chest was tight with fear.

Storm broke through the gap in the ice, spluttering for breath. Lucky felt dizzy with relief as she laid a paw on a shaft of ice, steadying herself. He was about to rush to her when a howl rose from the riverbank. He turned sharply to see Dagger looking as fearful as a pup, backing away from the bank and slamming into the other Fierce Dogs who had gathered around him to watch the fight.

"Blade has fallen!" Dagger gasped. "Our great leader is dead!"

Astonished barks echoed along the bank. "Blade has fallen! Blade is dead!"

Dagger shook his fur and seemed to calm down. "Come, Fierce Dogs! There is nothing for us here anymore." He spun away from the bank and started to march. The other Fierce Dogs fell into line, following the muscular dog into the forest. Only Mace stayed behind. The huge Fierce Dog, a bloody wound on the side of his neck, swayed on his paws a moment before rolling onto his side, his eyes gazing blankly into the sky as his breathing stilled.

Lucky threw a quick glance back at the river. Storm was starting to climb onto the ice that ran along the bank. He sighed with relief and turned to watch the Fierce Dogs retreat.

"Wait for me!" yelped a familiar voice.

An acid taste rose in Lucky's mouth as he spotted Whine creeping out from behind a tree. *He must have been hiding there all along,* Lucky thought with disgust.

The stout little dog scampered after the retreating Fierce Dogs. "Dagger! Let me come too, I can help you!"

Through the tumbling snow, Lucky could just see Dagger pause. Blade's former deputy didn't even bother to turn around. "You are *nothing*, runt-dog," he snarled. "Take one step closer and I'll show you how little your help means to us." The Fierce Dog started moving again, leading his Pack into a red horizon.

Whine froze, glancing about uncertainly.

Sweet stepped toward him, her muzzle rising over her fangs. "Get away!" she barked. "You're not welcome here, *traitor.*"

Sunshine ran out from behind the rocks. She rushed to Sweet's side, yipping angrily. Still Whine hesitated.

"You heard our Alpha! Get away from here!" Sunshine rushed at the goggle-eyed dog, baring her own small fangs. Whine gave a yelp and ran upstream as quickly as he could on his stumpy legs. Sunshine's tail wagged in satisfaction.

Lucky ran his tongue over his muzzle. He could not feel sorry for the little dog. *He betrayed the Pack. . . . He asked for this.*

A loud crack sounded from the river, and Lucky turned back to Storm with a whine. She was almost at the bank, but the ice was splitting beneath her. *I thought she was out!* he thought, horror-stricken. *Why didn't I go to help her?*

As he watched helplessly, the ice collapsed under Storm's weight. Struggling and splashing, she sank beneath the surface of the river again. Panic surged through Lucky's limbs. *This can't happen!*

He shuffled forward, keeping low on his belly. He reached out, stretching his neck, catching Storm's scruff between his teeth as she paddled desperately, but he was too weak to pull her out. She slipped out of his reach and disappeared under the water.

"She mustn't die," Lucky whimpered. His paws were tingling. The thumping of rabbits' feet in his head was so strong that he could no longer hear the dogs barking all around him. Through a haze, he saw Sweet, Rake, Whisper, and Moon run to the edge of the water. Bella left his side to join them, and Arrow hurried to help, his dark head disappearing beneath the water.

Lucky stared at them, pleading with his eyes. Leashed Dogs, Wild Dogs . . . Twitch's Pack . . . even a Fierce Dog. Coming together to save young Storm. *They won't let her drown. They can't. . . .*

He was confident of this, he realized. Storm would be saved.

The tingling from his paws crept over his body. As his eyes shut, he pictured the snowscape as he'd seen it for an instant, with a dazzling glow lighting up the trees.

CHAPTER TWENTY-THREE

Lucky limped up the hill toward the cliffs. Behind him the Endless Lake whooshed and sighed, beating its waves against the sand. The snow had finally stopped falling, but it had left behind its thick white pelt. Snow covered the deep banks of the lake, the tops of the longpaw buildings in the distant town, and the jagged contours of the cliffs. The air was clear and biting cold.

Sweet fell back, waiting for Lucky. She nuzzled his ear. "Are you okay, my Beta?"

He licked her muzzle, his tail wagging gently. "I'll be fine once I've had some sleep."

Sweet's Pack trooped slowly over the icy rocks, edging their way back to their camp. Twitch's Pack walked alongside them, exhausted but triumphant. Lucky's eyes trailed to Storm. She strode forward with her head raised high, despite her injuries.

He glanced up at the sky. The Moon-Dog was hidden behind a bank of cloud, but her gentle light glowed through, turning the air silvery. *We did it! We won the Storm of Dogs.* The half wolf was dead, and the River-Dog had taken Blade. The Fierce Dogs had fled, fearful as pups. *Blade was wrong about Storm—wrong about the third Growl.*

He climbed the last rock so he was standing at the top of the slope, at the borders of their camp, and pressed his paw against the snowy ground. Beneath its icy touch he felt the firm, solid presence of Earth-Dog. The Spirit Dog was sleeping peacefully. When Ice Wind passed, and Tree Flower arrived, new shoots would spring from the ground. Buds and blossom would unfurl in the trees, and birds would fill the air with song. Lucky could sense the promise of the future as a warmth in his chest, just as he had in his dream.

The dogs gathered beneath a huddle of low trees, deep in the Wild Dogs' camp, pressing together for warmth. Sweet addressed Twitch, her muzzle low as a mark of respect. "I know all in my Pack join me in sharing our deepest gratitude for your help." Lucky and the other dogs murmured their agreement, and Sweet continued,

"Your Pack is honorable and loyal. I am very sorry about Splash." She turned to Chase from Twitch's Pack. One of the small dog's eyes was swollen shut, and Lucky wondered if she would be able to use it again.

Sweet sighed. "Some of your injuries are grave. You have made a great sacrifice for us, and for the freedom of Wild Dogs everywhere."

Twitch dipped his head in acknowledgment. "We were honored to fight alongside you. You are a strong leader, Sweet. I know my Pack was inspired by your courage. We shall grieve for our lost Beta, and also for Martha, who fought so bravely to the last."

Storm whimpered and nuzzled against Lucky, who licked her ears. A great sadness burned in his chest as he thought of the water-dog. *She's safe now with River-Dog,* he reminded himself. He remembered Martha's quiet determination to belong, in the early days after the Big Growl, when he and the Leashed Dogs left the city. At first she had seemed so serious and restrained, but all that had changed when she'd first set eyes on the river. She had bounded in with so much excitement, just like a pup, paddling her webbed paws. She had always felt at home in the water—close to the River-Dog.

Twitch lowered himself onto his belly. "I've been thinking.

Our Packs work so well together—we are natural allies. More than that, we are friends."

There was a murmur of agreement from the gathered dogs.

Twitch's whiskers flexed as he spoke. "I don't think my Pack should go back to the forest." He met Sweet's gaze with his soft brown eyes. "Would you accept us into your Pack? We promise to be loyal to you, to obey your leadership and command in all things."

Lucky yipped happily, and Sweet rose to her paws. "Of course you can join us," she said, tail wagging.

Twitch rolled onto his back, exposing his belly in a gesture of submission. Sweet stepped forward, brushing his chest with a forepaw. Then she backed up a few paces and allowed Twitch to rise.

He raised his muzzle, standing nobly on three legs. "Thank you, Alpha." His Packmates broke into a volley of cheerful barks, and the Wild Dogs joined in.

When they quieted down, Sweet turned to Arrow. "You too are welcome to stay," she told the young Fierce Dog. "You acted heroically in the face of Blade's madness. I hope you will be happy in my Pack."

Arrow shuffled down onto his belly, his head on the ground.

He spoke in a grave voice. "Thank you, Alpha. I will do as I am told and make every effort to prove my loyalty to you. You too, Beta."

Lucky cocked his head at him. *Thank the Sky-Dogs, our faith in Arrow was not misplaced.*

Bella reached out a golden forepaw and batted the young dog playfully around the ears. "There's no need to be so fretful and serious. Sweet isn't a tyrant like Blade, and Lucky is *nothing* like Mace or Dagger!" Her tail started thrashing. "Sweet's a wonderful Alpha, and Lucky is the best kind of dog, believe me."

Lucky's chest swelled with pride as he watched his mate and his litter-sister exchanging respectful glances. His tail was wagging too.

Mickey sprang to his paws with a bark. "Prey! I can smell it!" He started digging wildly, just where he stood. The dogs sniffed around him eagerly.

"He's right!" barked Bruno, joining to kick back dirt.

Snap leaped at the widening hole, wiggling her small body through the gap. A moment later, her head appeared. "Rabbits!" she gasped.

The rich, earthy scent of rabbit fur filled Lucky's nostrils, and he licked his chops. He stepped out of the way, too exhausted to help. He watched as the hunters sprang into action.

Moon, Rake, and Bella darted out from between the trees, sniffing for an exit to the warren as Snap dug furiously, her agile body burrowing deep into the soil. She howled in triumph as three plump rabbits burst out of the hole between the trees. Finding themselves surrounded by dogs, the rabbits zigzagged chaotically. Mickey and Bruno seized a couple, snapping their necks with quick, firm jerks. Four more rabbits exploded from an exit to the warren in the snow where Bella, Rake, and Moon were waiting. One struggled free of Moon's grasp as she snorted in frustration, and another burst out over the snow and hopped to freedom. But Bella and Rake caught two of the rabbits and added their warm bodies to the pile.

"It's a sign from Earth-Dog," Sweet announced. "She is pleased with us and wants us to stay and make our home here, high above the Endless Lake."

The dogs yapped in agreement, wagging their tails.

Lucky's belly groaned in anticipation. Four large rabbits was a feast this deep into Ice Wind. The dogs turned to Sweet, waiting for her to eat her fill first, as was her right.

Sweet shoved a couple of rabbits toward Twitch, Bruno, and Daisy, who were sitting nearby. "Every dog fought hard today. I will not stand on ceremony—not now. Tonight, we eat together."

Lucky panted cheerfully, his chest glowing with affection for Sweet. It was the right decision—the dog-wolf would never have done that. Lucky's body tensed when he thought of the Pack's old leader, but he forced himself to relax. . . . *There is no point bearing grudges,* he told himself. *He paid for his treachery. He will have the Spirit Dogs to answer to now—it is not for me to judge him after he has passed.*

The dogs tucked into the rabbits. The sound of crunching bones and enthusiastic growls floated on the evening air.

Beetle ran his tongue over his dark muzzle. "I still can't believe how bravely Storm fought," he uttered, addressing his litter-sister in hushed tones.

"She really is some kind of Spirit Dog!"

Thorn's eyes were round with wonder. "She used the power of Earth-Dog and River-Dog to kill Blade!"

Lucky glanced at Storm. It was obvious the young Fierce Dog had overheard. She shifted from paw to paw, refusing to meet Lucky's gaze.

She's embarrassed, he realized. It was easy to forget that Storm was the same age as Beetle and Thorn. Despite her courage and vigor, she was scarcely more than a pup herself.

He huddled closer to her. "Don't mind them gossiping. I know the truth—you beat Blade through your own skill and determination."

Storm's ears dropped, and her tail gave a little wag.

Lucky nibbled at his forepaw, cleaning it of the last of the rabbit meat. He knew his words to Storm would reassure her, but secretly he had his suspicions. *She was so certain as she confronted Blade on the ice—almost like a Spirit Dog was speaking through her.*

At least there would be no more discussion of whether Storm belonged in their Pack. *No dog belongs here more,* Lucky mused. *She's proven her courage and loyalty many times over. She's already gone far, and her journey is just beginning. I wouldn't be surprised if I ended up calling her Alpha one day.*

The clouds dispersed and the Moon-Dog appeared, full and bright. Sweet called the Pack into the heart of the valley, where the snowy ground curved up to a ridge. There the Pack stood together, sharing the Great Howl. Lucky looked around at the faces, some old, some new . . . Bella, Mickey, Storm, Twitch, Sunshine, Whisper, and all the other dogs.

Warmth spread through his paws, and his body became light. He felt an intense connection with his Packmates, who had struggled so hard to survive, and who had fought off the Fierce Dogs together.

As the Howl grew louder, the dogs around Lucky faded from his view, and a gentle haze rose over the snowcapped valley. Four Spirit Dogs appeared through the mist: Sky, Forest, River, and Earth. They were there, protecting the Pack. And beside them, four pups. The pups Lucky had dreamed of. His breath caught as the dark brown pup raised her head and stared right at Lucky for a moment before fading from view.

Lucky let out a long breath, allowing the warmth and kinship of the Howl to glide over him. He pictured the Spirit Dogs gamboling over the valley, tumbling toward a forest of lush green trees. A group of dogs pranced after them. Lucky's head felt light as he recognized Alfie, Mulch, Spring, and Splash. Fiery strode after them, a tiny ball of fur bouncing along at his side—his and Moon's lost pup, Fuzz. Then Martha appeared, diving and bowing in the long grass, spinning and running with playful abandon. She made as if to follow the other dogs, then paused. A black-and-tan pup came waddling over the snow. He climbed onto the grass on his stout legs. His tail wagged so furiously when he saw Martha that his whole body moved from side to side.

Wiggle . . .

Martha greeted the pup with an affectionate lick, and together they followed Alfie, Fiery and Fuzz, Mulch, Spring, and Splash.

Lucky's old friends ran with the Spirit Dogs. They headed away from the deep snow of Ice Wind, over the grass where the sun of Long Light always shone.

The Howl broke off.

"Look!" barked Twitch. "Over the Endless Lake—there's a beam of light!"

Lucky and the other dogs trod over the snow and approached the cliff, careful to avoid the edge where the soil had fallen away. Sure enough, a bright light was sweeping across the lake and flashing over their camp.

"What can it mean?" Whisper murmured.

Moon's eyes glowed luminous blue beneath its gaze. "Maybe it's a message from the Spirit Dogs."

Lucky remembered a dazzling light, down on the water where the Fierce Dogs had rounded on them. "I think it's from the tall striped building—the one near the rocks." He recalled how the building had stood alone, overlooking the restless water.

"Does it mean the longpaws are coming back?" asked Bella.

Storm's floppy ears pricked up. "It isn't the longpaws. It's Martha, watching over us, like she said she would."

Maybe both are true, thought Lucky. *The longpaws may try to come back, now that the Earth Dog has found peace once again. But the Pack is strong.*

We will be all right. He gazed at the light as it continued its sweep over the lake. *Whatever happens, I know Martha will keep her promise—she will always watch over Storm and our Pack.*

The light cut out, but it wasn't dark on the cliff top. The Moon-Dog was still there, floating peacefully in the cool, clear sky. Lucky felt warm with his Pack huddled around him. He gave Storm a lick on the ear and turned to Sweet, who had curled up next to him. *Should I tell her that I have seen visions of our pups?* he wondered, longing to see them again.

He nuzzled closer to Sweet but didn't speak. He sensed that the time for words had passed, at least for that night. Soon the Sun-Dog would rise over a bright new day. Bulbs were twitching in the earth beneath the deep snow. Although the trees in the camp were stark and lifeless, buds would awaken along their branches as the air grew warmer. Suddenly Lucky was certain— when Tree Flower came, their pups would arrive.

Bella met his eye and blinked happily at him. Lucky blinked back. He could hear the rolling surf below as the lake swept up and down along the sand. His time as a Lone Dog felt like it was a lifetime ago, before the Growl scared the longpaws away and changed the world forever. Maybe one day the longpaws would return and things would be different. But for now, there was no one to disturb the Wild Dogs. They were free to hunt and rest as they chose; free to live by their own rules.

Lucky closed his eyes, feeling the comfort of his Pack, hearing their snuffles and snores as they drifted to sleep. He had a territory of his own now, and his friends were safe around him.

It was all he had ever really wanted.

ALSO BY ERIN HUNTER:
SURVIVORS

SURVIVORS: THE ORIGINAL SERIES

The time has come for dogs to rule the wild.

SURVIVORS: BONUS STORIES

Paperback

Download the three separate ebook novellas or
read them in one paperback bind-up!

HARPER
print of HarperCollinsPublishers

www.survivorsdogs.com